Praise for the delightful mysteries of

Kate Kingsbury . . .

"A charming cast of characters."   —*Literary Times*

"Sitting Marsh and its array of small-town citizens are realistically and humorously depicted."   —*The Mystery Reader*

"Likable characters, period details, and a puzzle that kept me guessing until the end . . . Very enjoyable."
                                                    —*Mystery News*

"Clever and cunning . . . Delightfully unique and entertaining. A most delicious tea-time mystery with just the right atmosphere and a charming cast of characters."
                                                    —*Literary Times*

"Delightful and charming."   —*Painted Rock Reviews*

"Always most enjoyable."   —*I Love a Mystery*

"Well-drawn characters."   —*Publishers Weekly*

"Full of humor, suspense, adventure, and touches of romance . . . delightful."   —*Rendezvous*

"A fun-to-read historical mystery."   —*Midwest Book Review*

"Trust me, you will not be disappointed . . . Ms. Kingsbury has created a memorable series with original characters that can be enjoyed over and over . . ."   —*Myshelf.com*

"Sublime . . .   . . . mystery."
                                                         —*BookBrowser*

Manor House Mysteries by Kate Kingsbury

A BICYCLE BUILT FOR MURDER
DEATH IS IN THE AIR
FOR WHOM DEATH TOLLS
DIG DEEP FOR MURDER
PAINT BY MURDER
BERRIED ALIVE
FIRE WHEN READY

FIRE WHEN READY

KATE KINGSBURY

BERKLEY PRIME CRIME, NEW YORK

THE BERKLEY PUBLISHING GROUP
Published by the Penguin Group
Penguin Group (USA) Inc.
375 Hudson Street, New York, New York 10014, USA
Penguin Group (Canada), 10 Alcorn Avenue, Toronto, Ontario M4V 3B2, Canada
(a division of Pearson Penguin Canada Inc.)
Penguin Books Ltd., 80 Strand, London WC2R 0RL, England
Penguin Group Ireland, 25 St. Stephen's Green, Dublin 2, Ireland (a division of Penguin Books Ltd.)
Penguin Group (Australia), 250 Camberwell Road, Camberwell, Victoria 3124, Australia
(a division of Pearson Australia Group Pty. Ltd.)
Penguin Books India Pvt. Ltd., 11 Community Centre, Panchsheel Park, New Delhi—110 017, India
Penguin Group (NZ), Cnr. Airborne and Rosedale Roads, Albany, Auckland 1310, New Zealand
(a division of Pearson New Zealand Ltd.)
Penguin Books (South Africa) (Pty.) Ltd., 24 Sturdee Avenue, Rosebank, Johannesburg 2196,
South Africa

Penguin Books Ltd., Registered Offices: 80 Strand, London WC2R 0RL, England

This is a work of fiction. Names, characters, places, and incidents either are the product of the author's imagination or are used fictitiously, and any resemblance to actual persons, living or dead, business establishments, events, or locales is entirely coincidental.

FIRE WHEN READY

A Berkley Prime Crime book / published by arrangement with the author

PRINTING HISTORY
Berkley Prime Crime mass-market edition / December 2004

Copyright © 2004 by Doreen Roberts Hight

ISBN: 0-425-19948-7

Berkley Prime Crime Books are published by The Berkley Publishing Group,
a division of Penguin Group (USA) Inc.,
375 Hudson Street, New York, New York 10014.
The name BERKLEY PRIME CRIME and the BERKLEY PRIME CRIME design are trademarks belonging to Penguin Group (USA) Inc.

PRINTED IN THE UNITED STATES OF AMERICA

10 9 8 7 6 5 4 3 2 1

CHAPTER

❁ 1 ❁

"After all the trouble that munitions factory has caused, I can't believe it's actually going to open this week." Violet slapped a kipper into the pile of flour on the breadboard. "Six months ago I'd have said that nice Mr. McNally was wasting his time."

Seated at the kitchen table, Lady Elizabeth Hartleigh Compton watched her housekeeper deftly turn the kipper until it wore a white coat of flour. "Douglas McNally certainly had a difficult fight on his hands. But then he's an assertive man, and very determined. Though I must say, I was surprised the councilors agreed to allow it."

"Money, that's what did it." Violet tossed the fish into the frying pan. A loud sizzle erupted as it hit the hot fat. "They can see it bringing money into the town. As for Fred

Shepperton, as soon as he found out how much that wily Scotsman was willing to pay to lease his land, he practically shoved it into the bugger's hands. Sold out to the devil, he did. That money won't do him any good, you mark my words. He's put a curse on all of us, that he has."

Elizabeth sighed. She'd heard the argument over and over again. The people of Sitting Marsh were violently opposed to having a munitions factory built so close to the village. Apart from the unwelcome eyesore marring the peaceful countryside, most of the villagers were convinced that the enterprise would make them a target for Hitler's bombs, which until now they had managed to avoid. McNally's visions of bringing more people into the area, creating houses, shops, schools, and work for everyone, only intensified the wrath of the residents.

Although Elizabeth could appreciate the economic benefits of the venture, she agreed wholeheartedly with the villagers' misgivings. Sitting Marsh was a quaint little village, and she hated the possibility of it becoming irreversibly changed by the advent of a modern factory.

On the other hand, she couldn't argue against the fact that such factories were vital to the war effort, and would certainly improve the income of the younger people, perhaps encouraging them to stay in the area instead of moving to the big cities.

"I thought Mr. McNally had given up," Violet said, breaking into Elizabeth's thoughts. "When he left here last year and went back to Glasgow I thought we'd never see him again."

"I understand he'd already come to an agreement with Fred Shepperton." Elizabeth rearranged her knife and fork, then straightened the triangle of white serviette. "Fred kept quiet about it all that time because he didn't want to upset the villagers if the venture fell through."

Martin, who had been sitting quietly reading the newspaper through the entire conversation, suddenly came to life. "If you ask me," he said, peering at Elizabeth over the top of his gold-rimmed specs, "I don't think the master is going to allow it."

Violet slapped another kipper into the pan. "Nobody asked you," she said rudely. "And in any case, since the master has been dead for God knows how long, I don't think anyone's going to be listening to him, either."

"I listen to him," Martin declared. "And what he says makes a great deal of sense."

"Which is more than I can say for you, talking to a bloody ghost." Violet slid a fried kipper onto a plate and carried it over to the table. "Here," she said, thrusting it in front of Elizabeth, "get that down you. You've been looking far too peaky lately. You need to get out of this house. Get some fresh air into your lungs."

Elizabeth looked at the offering without much enthusiasm. "I don't feel like going out. It's miserably cold out there. I don't think the snow is ever going to melt."

"Of course it will. Once the sun comes out again." Violet went back to the stove. "After all, the snow's only been on the ground since last week. It's not as if we've had it all winter. It'll soon melt once it warms up."

"Well, it's too cold to ride the motorcycle in this weather. Besides, where would I go? There's nothing to do if I do go out."

"Take yourself off to the pictures or something. There's a lot of good films on now."

Martin carefully folded up the newspaper. "I think that's

a jolly good idea, madam. You've been looking quite poorly lately. The master is worried about you."

"The master should be worrying about hisself," Violet said crisply. "Considering he's six feet under the cold ground."

"At least he has his wife to keep him company," Elizabeth muttered.

"I knew it." Violet flipped the fish over in the pan and turned to face her. "It's time you stopped pining after that American major, Lizzie. He's gone and that's that. You can't bring him back, so you might as well put him out of your mind and get on with your life."

She is right, Elizabeth thought mournfully. But knowing what was right and doing it were two different things. "He could have at least dropped me a line," she murmured. "Just to let me know how he's getting along."

"He sent a Christmas card, didn't he?"

"It wasn't a very personal message, was it." *Hope you all have a wonderful Christmas Season. Best Regards, Earl.* As if she were nothing more than a casual acquaintance. The emptiness she'd felt when she'd opened that long-awaited envelope was still an ache that kept her awake at night.

"Lizzie." Violet didn't often touch her physically, but she came over and draped a bony arm across her shoulders. "What did you expect? Major Monroe went back to his wife and family in America. His life is there. Yours is here. If you ask me, it was the best thing that could have happened for both of you when he was sent home. Though I'm sorry his son had to get hurt in that accident."

"At least Earl had the decency to let us know his son recovered. Except for the Christmas card, it's the only time he's written, and that was seven months ago."

Eight months since she'd seen him. Eight long, miserable,

lonely months, wondering how he was, what was happening to him. *If he'd patched things up with his wife.*

That was what really bothered her. Because to know that Earl was back with his wife was to give up all hope. Not that she deserved to hope for anything. After all, she'd been no more than Earl's landlady, and a reluctant one at that, when the war office had ordered her to open up the mansion to American officers stationed at the nearby base.

At first, her friendship with the handsome major had been tentative at best, but over the long months they had grown close. As close as was possible for a divorced lady of the manor and a USAAF major with a wife and family in America.

There had been many times when she'd longed to ignore the conventions and standards with which she'd been brought up to preserve at all costs. She had fought the temptations, striving to protect her precious reputation and the responsibilities she owed to the people of Sitting Marsh.

These were troubled times, and her villagers needed her now as never before. Facing the threat of invasion, or destruction from Hitler's bombs, the miseries of shortages and rationing, the possibility of their menfolk dying on a battlefield in a country they'd never seen, they needed someone to look up to—some reminder that all was not lost, and that the traditions and heritage they fought to maintain were still alive and well.

She'd reminded herself of that over and over this past year. A small part of her, however, wished now that she'd not been so stalwart in her protection of her reputation. Deep down inside, she wished that just once she'd given in to the longing in her heart. For now she would never know how it would be to love and be loved by Major Earl Monroe.

"Anyhow, you'll have to go out for the opening ceremony

of the factory. Seeing as how you're the guest of honor." Violet brought her kipper over to the table and sat down. "I hope you've got your speech all ready. Day after tomorrow, isn't it?"

Elizabeth poked at the offending fish with her fork. She wasn't that fond of fish for breakfast, but it was a change from a dreary bowl of porridge. How she missed the big breakfasts of the past, when the mansion was bustling with servants and guests. A full plate of bacon, eggs, sausage, fried tomatoes, fried bread, fried mushrooms, and buttered toast with maybe a small helping of fried roes every morning certainly gave one the energy to face the day. No wonder she was depressed. Kippers and porridge. Not much in the way of substitutes.

"Lizzie? You do have your speech ready, don't you?"

Pulling her thoughts back to the present, Elizabeth said listlessly, "I'll work on it today. I really have to be in the mood to write a decent speech. Polly used to help me write them, but she's been impossible ever since her boyfriend was transferred back to the States. I can't get her to concentrate on anything anymore. She used to be such a competent assistant."

"Well, at least she has a good excuse." Violet's thin features arranged themselves into a frown of disapproval.

Elizabeth bit back a retort. Violet never had approved of her friendship with Earl Monroe, even though she had assured her housekeeper over and over again that it was all very innocent. They had argued over it many times, and now that Earl was gone, Elizabeth had no intention of carrying on the argument.

She often wondered what her parents would say to hear Violet talking to the lady of the manor in such a tone. Or, for that matter, how they would react to the sight of their only daughter taking her meals with the servants in the kitchen.

The truth was, ever since her parents had died in a bombing raid on London, and her ex-husband had gambled away the family fortune, Elizabeth had lived more like a servant than the sole heir to the Wellsborough estate. What with the debts, the much needed repairs, the loneliness of the cold, vast mansion, all made even more miserable by an unusually bitter winter, she was seriously tempted to sell the estate and move back to London. Bombs notwithstanding.

The door burst open just then, shattering her thoughts. Sadie Buttons charged into the room, her round face flushed with excitement. Her mousy brown hair stuck out in a bunch on either side of her head like donkey ears and she clutched a feather duster to her chest as she halted in front of Elizabeth. "Guess what Polly just told me," she said, her voice shrill with excitement.

Violet gave her a look that would have stopped Hitler's army from advancing. "In case you have forgotten," she said icily, "it's customary to greet her ladyship before bellowing like an angry bull."

Martin's eyes gleamed with approval. "About time you reminded the pesky girl about her manners. Her mouth is as big as Blackwell Tunnel. I've never been witness to such deplorable behavior in a subordinate in all my years in the manor."

" 'Ere, who you calling a subordinate?" Sadie demanded.

"He means an employee, Sadie," Elizabeth said, giving Violet a slight shake of her head. Servants were hard enough to come by these days, and in spite of her unfortunate rebellious nature, Sadie was a very good housemaid. Efficient, hardworking, and loyal. One could hardly ask for more. Unless it was a less abrasive attitude, perhaps. In any case,

Elizabeth was prepared to make allowances rather than go through the dismal and quite impossible process of finding a more pliable applicant for the job.

Unfortunately, Violet wasn't as accommodating. She pushed her chair back, rose to her feet, and glared up at Sadie's flushed face. "You listen to me, young lady. You go out the door and you come back in the way you're supposed to do, with respect and consideration for her ladyship. If you do not, you will go without breakfast this morning. Is that clear?"

Sadie let out her breath in a rush of hot air. "Oh, all right. Sorry, your ladyship."

The door swung closed behind her, while Elizabeth murmured, "That really isn't necessary, Violet. The girl was excited about something, that's all."

"She has to follow the rules, Lizzie," Violet said firmly. "Otherwise we'll never be able to control her. She treats you like you're one of us." She carried her empty plate over to the sink and dumped the remains of her breakfast into the wastebin.

Elizabeth had to smile. "You can't blame her for that. Apart from the title, and all the responsibilities, which heaven knows I didn't want or ask for, I am no different than you or anyone else in the village."

Violet spun around and her frizzy hair seemed charged with electricity as she uttered a shocked gasp. "Lady Elizabeth Hartleigh Compton, how dare you say such a thing! After the upbringing you had, your aristocratic background, your place in the gentry, how can you lower yourself to the level of a commoner? Your father would turn in his grave to hear you say such a thing."

"I told you he was displeased with you, madam," Martin said smugly.

Violet turned on him. "Shut up, you old fool."

Elizabeth sighed. "My mother was a kitchen maid, who happened to marry an earl," she reminded Violet. "Something that some of the villagers will never let me forget."

"If you're talking about that snotty-nosed Rita Crumm," Violet said crossly, "who takes any notice of her? She's a pompous idiot with an inflated opinion of herself. She'd give her firstborn child to be in your shoes."

"Not if she knew the problems I have to deal with," Elizabeth said drily.

"That's what I wanted to tell you," an agitated voice said from the doorway.

Having totally forgotten about Sadie, Elizabeth swung around in her chair to look at her housemaid. "What is it, Sadie? What's happened?"

Sadie came forward and sent a sly glance at Violet before saying, "Good morning, your ladyship."

"Good morning, Sadie. Now tell me, what is it that has you in such turmoil this morning?"

"Probably lost her keys down the toilet," Martin mumbled and he laid his knife and fork down on his plate. "There are far too many bones in this kipper, Violet. I think I have one stuck in my throat."

"Doesn't stop you bleating though, does it." Violet snatched up his plate. "How do you think fish swim around if they don't have bones? If you don't behave yourself, Martin Chezzlewit, I'll take back the glasses I got for you after you gave yours away to that raffle ticket woman."

"I wish you would stop referring to Beatrice Carr as that raffle ticket woman." Martin glared at Violet over his specs. "You know very well what her name is and I wish you would use it."

"Chezzlewit?" Sadie said, looking amused. "Blimey,

what a bloody handle. No wonder you never use it." She winked at Martin. "I'd get rid of that, mate, if I was you."

Martin opened his mouth to reply, but Elizabeth hurriedly jumped in. "Sadie, if you want some breakfast I suggest you sit down and tell us what excited you so this morning."

"Oh, right, m'm." Sadie dragged a chair out from the table and plopped down on it. "What we got for breakfast? Kippers! Ooh, luvly. Me favorite they are. Can I have two?"

Violet rolled her eyes and went back to the stove, while Elizabeth said gently, "Sadie?"

"Right, m'm." Sadie leaned forward, her eyes gleaming with excitement. "Well, Polly heard it from Alfie, while she was down the pub last night."

Elizabeth interrupted her with an exclamation of surprise. "Polly went to the Tudor Arms last night? That *is* good news. She must finally be recovering from Sam Cutter's departure. I think this is the first time she's been out socially since he left."

"She must be getting over 'im," Sadie agreed. " 'Cos she's got a new boyfriend. I haven't met him yet, but Polly says—"

"Sadie!" Violet's harsh voice made them both jump. "Will you please stop repeating gossip to her ladyship and get to the important news as she asked."

Sadie rolled her eyes in an expression that would have intensified Violet's wrath had the housekeeper not had her back turned. "Well, m'm, it's them daft women in the Housewives League. They're planning a protest demonstration at the opening of the factory on Saturday. They say as how nobody's going to take that tour of the building unless it's over their dead bodies."

Violet clicked her tongue in annoyance. "Whatever

next! Those women should be ashamed of themselves, that they should. Behaving like a bunch of children, they are. Naughty ones at that. Disgusting, I call it. Fancy disrupting honest, hardworking people like that."

"Well, since you fail dismally in that category," Martin said from behind his newspaper, "obviously they won't be disrupting you, so there's no need to get in a frenzy about it."

Violet swung around. "Who asked you, you old goat?"

Ignoring them, Elizabeth stared at Sadie in dismay. "Oh, dear, I was rather afraid something like this would happen. Did Polly say what kind of demonstration?"

Sadie shook her head, making the bunches of hair flap back and forth. "No, m'm. Polly says it's all supposed to be a big secret, but Marge Gunther let it slip. You know what a big mouth Marge has got."

"That appears to be an epidemic around here," Martin grumbled.

"Well then, I'll talk to Polly about it. She might be able to tell me something that will help." Elizabeth dabbed at her mouth with her serviette, then laid it on the table. "I can't stop the Housewives League from demonstrating, but if I know what to expect, I might be able to prevent things from getting out of hand."

"Well, don't rely on the police constables to help." Violet slapped a plate of kippers in front of Sadie, glaring at the girl when she rudely smacked her lips. "You know how blinking useless they are. I swear George and Sid are afraid of Rita Crumm."

"Everyone's afraid of Rita Crumm," Sadie mumbled. "Bleeding old battle-axe."

Violet cuffed Sadie on the back of her head. "Watch

your language, my girl. And don't talk with your mouth full."

Elizabeth winced, but Sadie seemed not in the least bothered by Violet's outburst. She was too busy devouring her kippers.

"I'll be in the office if anyone needs me." Elizabeth headed for the door. *It's just as well,* she thought, *that Sadie is so easy-going. With her stocky build, she could send Violet's scrawny body across the kitchen with one sweep of her arm.* It was comforting to know that in spite of all the changes the war had brought to the world as they'd known it, the voice of authority still counted for something. She could only hope the same could be said when she was faced with the formidable group leader of the Housewives League.

She and Rita Crumm went back a long way, on a road fraught with contention. Their clashes were legendary, with Rita doing her very best to undermine the lady of the manor. The trouble with Rita was that she had ambition far beyond her capabilities. In charge of the war effort in Sitting Marsh, she often plunged into projects with more enthusiasm than common sense in her determination to be recognized as a leader. Her efforts sometimes brought admirable results. Other times, nothing short of disaster. This coming protest, for instance.

Elizabeth sighed as she climbed the creaking stairs to the upper floor of the drafty old mansion. A demonstration was the last thing Douglas McNally needed right now. Already facing a barrage of opposition to the new factory, this would only aggravate the villagers' concerns.

She would just have to appeal to Rita's patriotic ideals. After all, the factory would be a great asset to the war effort. According to the newspapers, the Allies badly needed more weapons and ammunition. Surely Rita would see the value in that.

Then again, when did that woman ever listen to reason? Unfortunately, it appeared very much as if yet another battle was brewing on the home front. And a nasty one at that.

CHAPTER

❈ 2 ❈

Polly sat at her desk, her chin slumped in her hands. She barely looked up as Elizabeth entered the office, and her voice sounded a little hoarse as she mumbled, "Good morning, your ladyship."

"Are you catching a cold?" Elizabeth peered at her young assistant in concern. "This dreadful weather is giving everyone a cold. Perhaps you should have stayed home today."

Polly shook her head and managed a weak grin. "It's not a cold, m'm. Honest. I was singing down the pub last night and lost me voice. It'll come back in a while, I'm sure."

"Well, at least it sounds as if you had a good time." Elizabeth sat down at her desk and started sorting through the pile of letters waiting for her attention. "Sadie tells me you have a met a young man," she said carefully.

Ever since Squadron Leader Sam Cutter had returned to America, Polly had been extremely sensitive on the issue of boyfriends. She seemed to brighten up quite a bit, however, when she answered.

"I met him at the Arms. His name is Ray Muggins, and he's down from London. Got a job at the new factory. He's training the women to work on the conveyor belts. He used to work at a factory in London, so he knows what he's doing." She sent Elizabeth a sly smile. "He's awfully handsome. Reminds me of Humphrey Bogart, he does."

Elizabeth paused. "Well, I hope he's younger than Humphrey Bogart." It was rather a personal comment, she reflected belatedly. Then again, a significant age difference had caused the breakup of Polly's romance with the American officer. She wouldn't want to see the girl hurt again like that.

Polly's smile wavered. "He's younger than Sam, if that's what you mean."

Immediately contrite, Elizabeth hurried to make amends. "I'm sure he's a very nice young man. In any case, it's really none of my business."

"He is really nice. He had some kind of illness when he was a baby and it gave him a bad heart. That's why he's not in the army. You'd never know it, though, to look at him. I really like him a lot."

Sensing the lack of confidence behind Polly's words, Elizabeth frowned. "Well, you have plenty of time to get to know him. I imagine he'll be staying here in Sitting Marsh for a while if he's going to train the factory workers."

"He's nice-looking, he's got plenty of money, and he makes me laugh. That's all I need to know, m'm."

Deciding that she'd already said enough, Elizabeth changed the subject. "Well, I have to write a speech for the opening ceremony for the factory, so I'd better get on with it. Sadie tells me you heard that the Housewives League was planning a protest. Did Alfie say exactly what they had in mind?"

Polly shook her head. "Sorry, m'm. I don't think he knew much about it. Marge started to tell him, but then she shut up. Afraid of what Rita Crumm would say, I reckon."

"No doubt," Elizabeth said grimly. "Well then, I shall just have to be prepared for anything." She watched Polly carry a handful of paid bills over to the file cabinet. Something in the girl's voice when she'd talked about her new boyfriend made her uneasy. She could only hope that Polly wasn't using this young man to get over her breakup with Sam Cutter. So many bad relationships were caused by acting on the rebound from a broken heart. She said no more about it, however, aware that Polly was unlikely to appreciate or heed her advice.

An hour later the office chores had been taken care of, and she sent Polly down to the village to collect an overdue rent. It was a task that Elizabeth thoroughly disliked, while Polly seemed to actually enjoy the chance to exercise her newly found assurance.

That was one thing Sam Cutter had done for her, Elizabeth thought, as the door closed behind her assistant. Polly was growing up. It was sad that she'd had to learn such a hard lesson so young, but perhaps it would save her from making an even more disastrous mistake. Like marrying the wrong man for the wrong reasons.

Irritated by the unwelcome memory of her former husband, Elizabeth pushed her chair back and wandered over to the window. Now that they were in the heart of winter, the daylight hours were short, making the long night of blackout even more depressing.

Maybe Violet was right. Maybe she should get out more. Being cooped up in this sprawling mansion with its dark walls and ancient furnishings was enough to make anyone feel dreary.

Outside the window, the snow-covered lawns swept down to the woods in a smooth, unbroken flow of white. Beyond them, scrawny, leafless limbs stabbed the metal skies with witchlike claws. In the distance, a sliver of silver gray ocean peeked through the bare trees. The North Sea looked as bleak as the sky.

Across a different ocean, Earl was under the same sky. It comforted her to remind herself of that. She missed him so much. Even though he'd been gone so many months, she could still picture him as clearly as if he'd just left. She could see him rocking in his favorite chair in the conservatory, a glass of Scotch in his hand, the blond streaks gleaming in his light brown hair.

Even after months of living in the cool English climate, his leathery skin had never quite lost the deep tan of a man used to being in the sun. She smiled to herself, remembering. But then, as always, the memories brought back the pain of losing him.

She turned away from the chilly view from the window and crossed the room to where the wicker rocking chair stood. Earl had sat in it so often he'd considered it "his" chair. After he'd left, she'd had Desmond, the gardener, bring it up to her office. She couldn't bear the thought of anyone else sitting in it now.

At times, when she ached with loneliness, she'd take comfort in sitting in the chair herself. She sat down on it now, leaned back, and closed her eyes. Rocking gently back and forth, she wrapped herself in the memory of Earl. The way his eyes crinkled at the edges when he smiled.

The strand of hair that fell across his forehead. His deep voice uttering her name, making it sound so much more romantic in his American drawl.

After a while she made herself get out of the chair. *All the imagining in the world wasn't going to bring him back,* she told herself sternly. She was simply delaying the process of forgetting him. Considering he was never hers to begin with, she was being quite silly about the whole thing.

Such self-reprimands had become a habit lately. Not that they solved anything, but at least she could tell herself she was making the effort.

Sighing, she sat down at her desk and pulled a notepad toward her. She had two days to write a speech that would reassure the villagers that the establishment of a munitions factory within the vicinity of Sitting Marsh did not amount to a horde of Nazi bombers dropping their deadly load on the village. A speech that would convince her people that the factory would bring many benefits, such as higher wages that would be spent in the town. A speech that would drown out that dratted woman, Rita Crumm, and silence her well-meaning but utterly dense followers. *In other words,* Elizabeth thought gloomily, *an impossible task.*

"So tell me more about this new bloke you met." Sadie sat on the bottom step of the stairs and gazed up at Polly in expectation. "How old is he? Where's he living? How long is he going to be in Sitting Marsh? Has he offered you a job?"

Polly tugged her arms out of her heavy overcoat. "What if he has?"

Sadie's jaw dropped. "Go on! You're not going to take him up on it, are you? What will her ladyship do without you?"

The other girl shrugged. "Don't know. I'm thinking

about it, though. It's more money than I'm making here, and now that Marlene's gone, Ma could use the extra shillings."

Sadie nodded. "Ain't that the truth. Have you heard from Marlene lately?"

"Not since Christmas." Polly pulled the wooly scarf from her head, letting her thick hair fall to her shoulders. "I still can't believe she's in Italy, driving an ambulance in the war zone. It's like a bad dream, it is. I don't think Ma's ever going to get over it. I hear her crying in the night sometimes, and I know she's afraid for our Marlene."

Sadie's eyes were full of sympathy. "You must miss her, too. What with your dad in the navy as well; that makes it twice as hard."

"Well, at least I don't have no one telling me how to dress and pinching me lipstick. The only thing I miss Marl for is her telling me if me seams are straight."

Sadie grinned. "Well, maybe your new boyfriend can help out there."

Polly pulled a face at her. "I've got to get back up to the office. I've got Mrs. Pettiscue's rent here, and her ladyship will be wondering what I did with it."

"Me, too. I've still got the Yanks' lavatories to clean." Sadie got to her feet. "If I don't get them done before they get back from the base, I'll never get in there. I never seen no one use toilets as much as them Yanks, I swear."

Polly nodded, her lips pressed tightly together. Any mention of the Americans billeted in the manor reminded her of Sam. Everything about the manor reminded her of Sam. She'd spent so much of her time hanging around the officers' quarters in the hopes of bumping into him. Now she did her best to avoid being anywhere near the east wing.

It was one of the reasons she was thinking about taking

a job at the factory. Maybe the biggest reason. Though she wasn't looking forward to telling Lady Elizabeth she was leaving. That was going to be hard all right. She stomped up the stairs, wondering why life had suddenly turned on her. Nothing seemed to go right lately. Nothing since Sam had left, anyway. Maybe working at the factory would help her feel better. That and Ray Muggins. It was nice to have a boyfriend again. Even if he wasn't Sam. Shoving away the tinge of doubt, she headed for the office.

The morning of the grand opening of Farnwell's Ltd. dawned with a scattering of snowflakes that quickly dispersed as the sun broke through the clouds. Aboard her motorcycle, bundled up in a thick wool reefer coat and white angora scarf, Elizabeth roared into the car park of the factory amid a greeting of applause and a whistle or two from the gathering crowd.

A quick glance around assured her that so far Rita Crumm and her entourage had not assembled, though she had no doubt it was only a matter of time. With one hand holding her skirt at a respectable angle, she climbed off the motorcycle and graciously waved at her villagers. Made up mostly of women, since all able-bodied men had been summoned to the war front, the small crowd waved back.

The building was quite unimpressive, Elizabeth decided. It was longer than the Manor House, but not as wide and only one floor. With its stark beige walls and tiny windows, it looked more like a prison camp than a factory. Although the official grand opening was today, the factory had already been in full production since before Christmas.

At each end of the building, a short flight of steps led up to an entrance. Standing in a doorway at one end, flanked by a couple of scared-looking young women, stood the sturdy figure of the man who had brought this controversial aberration to the picturesque countryside.

Elizabeth had first met Douglas McNally when he was scouting for suitable land for the factory. Although she had been against the project from the first, she rather liked the dour Scotsman. He spoke his mind, and she admired that. Too many people trod on eggshells around her, as if afraid to say the wrong thing.

That had been one of the things that had attracted her to Earl. Having been brought up in a country that had far less regard for class distinction, Earl had no compunction about saying what he thought, even if his opinion made gentle fun of her standing in society. It was refreshing, and oddly comforting.

He'd made her feel as if she were a woman, any woman—part of and accepted by the masses, enabling her to forget at times that she was an impoverished aristocrat with enormous responsibilities. It had all been rather wonderful.

Watching Douglas McNally hurry down the steps to greet her, Elizabeth thrust her memories from her mind. Right now she had far more important things with which to concern herself. She was becoming increasingly aware of a sound in the distance. A sound that could not be attributed to a passing vehicle. A sound that, if she wasn't mistaken, meant trouble.

Elizabeth smiled at McNally, trying to ignore the flutter of apprehension. She had dealt with Rita Crumm and her earnest band of followers plenty of times in the past. She would do so again. She could only hope that the man standing in front of her was as indomitable as he appeared. She would need all the help she could get.

"Lady Elizabeth!" Douglas McNally gave her a gentlemanly tilt of his head. "I'm so happy you are honoring us today with your delightful presence."

Elizabeth beamed at him. She had always enjoyed the way the Scots rolled their r's, and McNally's brogue was particularly pronounced. "Thank you, Mr. McNally. I have a short speech prepared. Where would you like me to stand?"

McNally nudged his head in the direction of the building. "At the top of the stairs, if ye will, your ladyship. We have a ribbon across the door, and a sharp pair of scissors for you to cut it."

Grateful that her companion had the foresight to sweep the snow from the front of the building, Elizabeth made her way to the steps and mounted them. She murmured a greeting to each of the young ladies, then turned to face the crowd. As she did so, the distant sound gradually intensified, drawing ever closer. She could identify it now. The crashing and banging of saucepans. Rita Crumm was on the march.

Tightening her lips, Elizabeth turned to face the hushed crowd. If she spoke really fast, she might be able to get the whole speech done before Rita's mob drowned her out. Heads were already turning in the direction of the racket, people murmuring among themselves.

"Ladies and gentlemen," Elizabeth began. "Behind me, in this building, arms and ammunition are being manufactured for the use of our military personnel fighting this dreadful war. This work presents a wonderful opportunity . . ."

She paused as the sound of crashing pans intensified enough to intrude. Out of the corner of her eye she saw a ragged procession of women enter the car park. They trudged behind the stork-like figure of Rita Crumm, who held a couple of saucepan lids like cymbals and marched with a ridiculous lift of her knees reminiscent of the German army's infamous goose step.

Rita, in fact, appeared to be the only one in the group with any animation. The rest of her troops looked ready to drop to the ground. Given that they had apparently marched all the way from the village, a distance of at least two miles, Elizabeth wasn't too surprised to see them so exhausted.

The procession made its way across the car park, heading for the steps where Elizabeth stood. The crowd drew back to let them pass, obviously intimidated by the large frying pans and heavy pots wielded by the bedraggled women, most of whom were listlessly banging their weapons with spoons.

Rita clashed her saucepan lids even louder as she reached the bottom of the steps and came to a defiant stop. "Halt!" she screamed.

She needn't have bothered. The women behind her, red-faced and puffing, had already decided they'd had enough. They had come to a full stop several yards behind their leader.

Rita glared at McNally, who stood slightly in front of Elizabeth as if ready to protect her against the wrath of the devil. "We are here," she bellowed, "to protest the opening of this factory on the grounds that it was built without taking into consideration the wishes of the people who live here and will have to put up with this . . ." She waved her hand at the offending building, then, apparently at a loss for a suitable description, added, ". . . despicable outrage. We charge that you, Mr. McNally, are subjecting the people of Sitting Marsh to extreme danger by erecting this. . . ."

Again she sought for a word and finally came up with one. ". . . monstrosity, thus inviting Hitler's bombs to destroy it, and all of us with it."

At her words a soft muttering of concern rippled through the crowd. Apparently Rita was less than pleased with the response. She turned to her stalwart followers and raised her hand sharply in the air to encourage them. A ragged cheer or two was all she could muster, however, and her scowl promised retribution for her troops later on.

Elizabeth held up her hand, and the murmuring died down. "Good morning, Rita," she said, when she was sure she had the attention of everyone. "How nice of you to bring such a turnout to our little ceremony."

Rita raised a trembling hand and, abandoning all attempts at good manners, pointed an accusing finger. "Shame on you, Lady Elizabeth! Shame on you for allowing this man to place the people of Sitting Marsh in the path of death and destruction. You, of all people, have betrayed us."

Beside her, McNally uttered a soft groan. "Oh, good God."

A louder murmur arose from the crowd, then died again as Elizabeth once more lifted her hand. "Please, everyone, listen to me. I admit I had my reservations about the factory at first. I agree that this building is a blight on the landscape. But after talking to Mr. McNally here, I am convinced that a year or two of inconvenience will be well worth the results. Our men and women in His Majesty's forces are in desperate need. There is only so much the government and the military can do. This isn't only their war, it is ours, too. Every man, woman, and child in this country is fighting for survival. If we are to win, if we are to beat back the terrible forces that seek to destroy us, if we are to save

England and restore our country to its former glory, then we must stand together, shoulder to shoulder, all for one and one for all."

Obviously stirred by this rousing call to arms, the crowd burst into cheers and wild applause, led with great enthusiasm by the Housewives League.

Rita waited, her cheeks growing red, for the din to die down. After a scathing glance at her disloyal army, she raised her voice again. "How can we stand shoulder to shoulder, if we're being blown to kingdom come by Hitler's bombs?"

More muttering greeted her words. A belated call came from her group of protestors. "You tell them, Rita!"

McNally stepped forward. "If I may—" he began, but boos from the crowd, drowned him out.

Elizabeth moved to stand beside him. "Let him speak," she commanded. "He has a right to defend his enterprise."

"Not if he's trying to get us all killed, he doesn't," Rita yelled back.

"I can promise," McNally roared above the growing rumble of dissent from the crowd, "Hitler won't even know we are here. We've camouflaged the roof, and as long as everyone keeps quiet about what we're doing here, he'll never know. Remember, loose lips sink ships."

"What if he does find out?" Rita demanded. "What then?"

McNally lifted his hands in appeal. "We're a very small enterprise compared to the big factories. The Germans are not going to risk getting shot down for a wee business like this one. Not with an airfield of American fighter pilots just a few miles away."

"He's right," Elizabeth added. "The Americans are

always on the alert for enemy planes, as is the British Army in Beerstowe. We have all the protection we need."

This time the muttering from the crowd seemed a little less hostile. Apparently sensing she was losing the fight, Rita rallied once more to the cause. "What about the people working here? Who's going to take care of things in the village if everyone's working in this place?"

"A lot of the workers are from North Horsham," McNally answered. "Not too many are from Sitting Marsh. Certainly not those who are needed in the village, I'm sure."

Doubting voices were raised once more from the worried throng.

Elizabeth decided it was time for her final argument. "Just think," she called out, "what this could mean. The rifle that is made here next week could save the life of your husband. The machine gun this factory produces could prevent a massacre in the trenches that are sheltering your sons. This is our chance to contribute to the war effort in a far more meaningful way than has been possible before."

She gestured at Rita, who showed no sign of giving up. "Rita Crumm and her Housewives League have contributed so much with their knitting and their collection of milk bottle caps and cigarette wrappers. Their constant efforts are vastly appreciated by the government, I can assure you all of that. But now we have the chance to take this one step further. A huge step further. Now we can help to save lives. Now we can help to bring our men and women home. Isn't that worth putting up with an ugly building for a while?"

McNally, taking advantage of the crowd's indecision, spoke up. "It will only be for a year or two. Once the war is over, we can change it into something else. Maybe a theatre, or a club house where ye can all have some fun."

"Or pull it down," someone yelled.

"Yeah, it's too bloody ugly," someone else added.

"We'll remodel it," McNally promised them. "Once the boys come back from the war they'll be glad to give us a hand. Between us we'll make this building so grand no one will ever remember what it was before. We'll call it Victory Hall, or Victory Theatre, or whatever it turns out to be. It will stand as a memorial for all the sacrifices and hard work you people will have put into it."

The voices in the crowd were now tinged with excitement. Rita, however, was not about to give up. Shouting to be heard above the crowd, she yelled, "You haven't heard the last of this, Douglas McNally! We will not put our children in danger! We will not rest until we shut you down!" She gestured violently in the air and managed to raise a weak cheer from her group.

No one else appeared to be taking any notice of her, however. Seizing the moment, Elizabeth snatched the scissors from the hands of the terrified young girl who held them and snipped the blue ribbon in half.

Raising the gleaming shears above her head, she called out, "I now pronounce this establishment open. May all who work here be productive and happy. God bless England, and God save the King!"

"England and the King!" the crowd roared back.

"Thank heavens," Elizabeth said, handing the scissors to McNally. "I was afraid we were going to have a riot on our hands. We appear to have weathered that particular storm rather nicely."

"Maybe," McNally said, his face now grave. "I said nought about this before, ye ladyship, because I didna want to worry you. But I'm afraid there could be a bigger storm on the horizon."

Elizabeth stared at him in concern. "What do you mean?"

McNally gestured at the crowd. "What I mean," he said slowly, "is that someone out there wants rather desperately to see me dead and buried. And I have not the slightest doubt he means business."

CHAPTER

❈ 3 ❈

The shock of McNally's words took Elizabeth's breath away. "Surely you must be mistaken," she said, when she could finally speak again. "I know the villagers have concerns about the factory, but I find it difficult to accept that someone feels strongly enough about it to go to such great lengths as murder."

"Aye, I hope you're right." McNally looked over his shoulder to see if his two assistants were listening. After satisfying himself that they were engrossed in conversation with each other, he said quietly, "I've been getting letters. Pushed through my letterbox by someone's hand. They're not signed, and they all say the same thing: Pull down the factory or prepare to meet my Maker."

"Oh, dear. How very upsetting." Elizabeth struggled

with common sense. "I'm quite sure the letters are just an attempt to frighten you into closing down the factory. I have no doubt the author of them has no intention of carrying out such a ridiculous threat. People say a lot of things they don't mean when they are agitated about something."

"I hope you're right." McNally stared bleakly across the heads of the people milling around. "I just wish they could see the benefits of this business, instead of concentrating on the pitfalls. This factory will bring money into the town. New life. New opportunities. A chance for Sitting Marsh to grow and prosper."

Elizabeth sighed. "I'm afraid that's the problem. The older people don't want things to change. They like things the way they are."

McNally gave her a probing glance. "Is that how you feel, your ladyship?"

"I want what's best for my people." Elizabeth glanced up at the unsightly building. "I have to be honest, Mr. McNally. Right now, I'm not sure what that is."

"Well, it'll work out, you'll see." McNally rubbed his hands together. "Just wait until we get cracking on the production lines and the workers start bringing home those big paychecks. That'll change their minds in a hurry."

Elizabeth had her doubts on that score. A good many of the villagers considered money the root of all evil. But she kept her counsel for now. Time would indeed tell. And perhaps McNally was right. Perhaps new life was exactly what Sitting Marsh needed to bring it out of the dark ages and into a bright new future.

After bidding the Scotsman farewell, she made her way across the car park to where she'd left her motorcycle. As she approached, she saw the stocky figure of Captain Wally Carbunkle waving to her. She headed toward him, her heart sinking when she saw Rita Crumm standing at his side. She wished now she'd pretended not to notice Wally's greeting. Fortunately, the rest of Rita's entourage appeared to have dispersed, no doubt anxious to get back to the security of their homes.

Wally pulled his sea captain's cap from his head as she approached. He'd trimmed his normally bushy white beard and mustache and looked quite dapper. Rita seemed a little uneasy, her gaze darting everywhere except at Elizabeth when she paused in front of them.

"Your ladyship," Wally said, "that was a dandy speech. Got me right here." He jammed a thumb in his chest. "Very stirring. Aye, indeed."

"Thank you, Captain." Elizabeth did her best to ignore Rita, who was fidgeting with her gloves, pulling them on and off. "I hope I managed to ease some of the concerns of the villagers."

"Oh, I reckon you did at that." Wally beamed. "I've been trying to do a bit of that, myself, you know. Since I'm the new night watchman for the factory."

Elizabeth looked at him in surprise. "You're working for Mr. McNally?"

Wally puffed out his chest. "That's right, your ladyship. Mr. McNally needed someone for the job and I volunteered. After all, we can't be too careful now, can we. Very dangerous stuff going on in this establishment. McNally needs someone responsible to watch over it at night."

"Yes, indeed," Elizabeth murmured. "But I was under the impression you'd retired."

"From the sea, m'm, yes, I have." He leaned toward her and winked. "But now I'm getting married, I'm going to need a little extra, so to speak. I have to keep my bride in the manner to which she's been accustomed."

"Well, that shouldn't be too difficult," Rita said huffily.

Ignoring her, Wally smiled at Elizabeth. "Speaking of which, your ladyship, seeing as how Priscilla and me are taking the plunge, I was wondering if you'd do us the honor of attending our little ceremony. I know my little lady would be very happy to see you there."

"I'd be delighted to come to your wedding," Elizabeth said warmly. "Just give Polly all the details. I shall look forward to it."

"Thank you, Lady Elizabeth. Priscilla will be very pleased."

"Is it going to be a big wedding?" Rita asked loudly.

Wally started as if he'd forgotten she was there. "What? Oh, no, Mrs. Crumm. Not at all. Just a few close friends and relatives, that's all."

Rita smoothed her gloves on again. "I see." She glanced slyly at Elizabeth. "I hope you didn't take anything I said this morning personally, your ladyship."

"Of course not, Rita," Elizabeth said pleasantly. "You were stating your opinion, to which we are all entitled."

"Exactly." Rita tossed her head back, nearly dislodging the floppy felt hat she wore. "After all, I have only the best interests of the people at heart."

Suggesting I don't, Elizabeth fumed inwardly.

Rita turned to Wally. "I imagine you're inviting the *important* people of the village to your wedding?"

Wally seemed taken aback by the question. "Well, I hadn't really given it much thought—"

"Well, I should just like to say that as head of the House-wives League and, as her ladyship so truly pointed out, my efforts are greatly appreciated by the government, I think I have a place of standing in Sitting Marsh, do I not?"

Wally scratched his thick mane of white hair. "I suppose so, but—"

"Well, then?" Rita glared at him, while Elizabeth did her best to hide a smile. Poor Wally. He was no match for the formidable Rita.

"I . . . don't see . . . what . . . what . . ." he sputtered.

Obviously put out, Rita leaned forward and thrust her face close to his. "The wedding," she said, forming each word carefully. "I hope I can expect an invitation?"

"Oh!" Wally looked hopefully at Elizabeth, but there was little she could do to help.

Feeling sorry for him, she said brightly, "Well, I must be off. Duty calls and all that." Without waiting for a response, she set off toward her motorcycle. Just as she reached it she caught sight of a tall figure in the forest-green uniform of the American Army Air Force, and her heart turned over. The officer had his back to her and was talking to the young girls who had stood with McNally at the top of the stairs.

They were looking up at him and giggling. As if in a trance, Elizabeth watched them, conscious of her heart pounding in her side. Then the man turned to leave, and she saw at once it wasn't Earl. How could it be? Earl was thousands of miles away on a different continent.

She swung her leg across the saddle of the motorcycle as elegantly as she could manage, ever mindful that someone could be watching her. But her thoughts were on the young officer as he crossed the car park. She had to stop this, she told herself sternly. She had to stop seeing Earl's figure in every uniformed back. She had to stop watching for him, hoping he'd return. He hadn't said so in so many words, but he'd left her with the impression that he didn't expect to return to Sitting Marsh. In fact, he'd been replaced by another major—a somewhat boorish man who thankfully had declined the invitation to be billeted at the Manor House, opting instead to stay on the base.

Several of the officers staying at the manor had also expressed relief at the news that their new commanding officer wouldn't be staying in their quarters. They all missed Earl, who had been firm but approachable with his men.

None of them could possibly miss him as much as she did. Roaring down the High Street, Elizabeth blinked, telling herself it was the wind that brought the tears to her eyes. She was recovering from her ridiculous crush on Major Earl Monroe. The longer he was away, the less she remembered him. And if she kept telling herself that, one day it might actually be true.

It was a week later when the unthinkable happened. By then, thanks to a spell of warmer air coming in from the south, the snow had all but disappeared. Elizabeth had started taking the dogs for long walks now that the grass was visible again. George and Gracie, a gift from Earl and named by him, romped joyfully across the Downs, enjoying the long-awaited freedom.

Elizabeth loved to watch them play. Their bloodhound mix gave them ungainly legs and heads that seemed too big for their bodies, yet they managed to look incredibly graceful as they raced across the long grass. The dogs had been a huge comfort to her after Earl had left, as if he had left part of himself behind with them.

After tiring herself out one windy afternoon, she'd retreated early to her bedroom, planning to read a new novel she'd picked up in North Horsham earlier that week. As usual, however, reading made her sleepy, and after only a page or two into the book, she fell soundly asleep.

She awoke later to the sound of her door opening, and Violet's urgent voice. "Lizzie? Wake up. You have to get up. We've been bombed."

Elizabeth sat up, shaking the sleep from her mind. "Bombed? Where? At the manor?"

"No, of course not. You would have woken up long before this if we had. Have you got your blackout curtains closed?"

"Yes, of course. But . . ."

Violet switched on the light. She stood in the doorway, her frizzy hair standing on end. Obviously it had not received the benefit of a comb. One hand clutched the neck of her wool dressing gown, while in the other she held a torch, the beam of which swept the ceiling as she gestured with it. "Get up, Lizzie. The Germans have dropped a bomb on the factory."

"Oh, no!" Elizabeth threw back the covers and reached for her blue quilted dressing gown lying at the foot of her bed. "When? What happened?"

"I just heard the news from George. He's downstairs waiting for you. He's in such a dither, you'd never know he was a blinking policeman the way he's carrying on."

Elizabeth dragged on her dressing gown and squinted at the clock. "What's the time?"

"It's almost one o'clock. George says the bomb must have been dropped at about eleven. Fred Shepperton called him from the Tudor Arms. You'd think a farmer would have his own telephone, wouldn't you, instead of having to ride his bike down the coast road to the pub."

"I don't believe it." Elizabeth struggled to clear her mind. "How did German planes manage to find that building in the dark without being detected by the American base or the army camp?"

"Don't ask me. They must have all been asleep on duty over there."

Violet was shivering, but whether from cold or fright Elizabeth couldn't tell. She was cold herself, in spite of her heavy dressing gown. Their only source of heat was a coal fireplace, and her fire had long gone out, leaving the room as damp and chilled as the lawns outside.

"What about the American officers?" Elizabeth demanded, following her housekeeper to the stairs. "Did anyone wake them?"

"Not only woke them up, they're on their way to the base." Violet's face was white in the reflection from her torch.

"And Martin and Sadie?"

"In the kitchen. Martin's got the old blunderbuss from off the wall again. Won't let go of it. Keeps saying he's going down fighting."

"Oh, dear." Elizabeth wrapped the collar of her dressing gown closer around her neck. "I do hope he didn't load it."

"I doubt if it would fire even if he did. It's older than he is." Violet reached the bottom step and hurried toward the kitchen. "I left Sadie making a pot of tea. Though I don't know if we'll have time to drink it. We might have to evacuate the manor."

Not if I have any say in the matter, Elizabeth thought firmly. This was her home and no Nazi bomber was going to put her out of it.

Inside the kitchen, the light seemed all the brighter after the eerie glow of Violet's torch. Police Constable George Dalrymple sat at the table with Martin, both men sipping a cup of tea. As Elizabeth entered the room George dropped the cup back in the saucer and shot to his feet.

Martin's cup clattered into his saucer as well. He

struggled to rise, hampered by the clumsy firearm he clutched in one hand.

George nodded in Martin's direction. "I tried to take it off him, m'm. Refuses to give it up, he does."

"It's all right, George." Elizabeth gave Martin a reassuring smile. He looked particularly frail right then. The few straggly gray hairs on his head were tangled together, and he'd forgotten to put on his glasses. Instead of his usual neat attire of a crisp white shirt and tie, vest, and jacket, he wore a knitted cardigan—which had definitely seen better days—over his pyjama jacket. He kept blinking his watery eyes, as if he were trying to wake up from a bad nightmare.

"I'm sorry to disturb you this time of night, your ladyship," George said. "Thought you'd like to know what's going on."

"Yes, of course." Elizabeth glanced at Sadie, who stood by the stove, a steaming cup in her hands, her expression grim but resolved. Remembering that the housemaid had once been bombed out of her home in London, Elizabeth could only imagine what was going through her mind. Over in the corner, the two dogs lay watching everyone, obviously confused at being woken up at such an abysmal hour.

Elizabeth sat down at the table. "I can't believe we didn't hear the planes. Did the siren go off? Why didn't we hear it?"

"I don't think anyone spotted them." George glanced at Martin, as if waiting for him to sit down first. "I'll have to have a word with our night watchmen. I don't know who's turn it is tonight, but he must have been asleep on the job, that's all I can say."

"That's what I said," Violet muttered.

"When exactly did this happen?" Elizabeth demanded. "Is it just the factory? How bad is it? Was anybody hurt?"

Without saying a word, Martin began the process of re-seating himself.

George followed suit, and she could tell by his expression that the news wasn't good. "I came straight from the factory to tell you, m'm. The firemen were putting out the fire when I left." He fiddled with the handle of his cup, avoiding looking at her. "We reckon the bomb were dropped somewhere around eleven o'clock this evening. It took out the east end of the building and set fire to the rest." He rattled the teaspoon in his saucer. "They found two people in there, m'm. Locked inside the office, they were."

Elizabeth caught her breath. "Who were they?"

"Mr. McNally was one of them. He was working late, it seems." George sighed. "Jessie Bandini was the other one. She cleans the office and the canteen in the evenings. She must have been just about ready to go home when it hit." He passed a hand over his balding head. "Poor Jessie. Her daughter's going to miss her, that's for sure."

"She's dead?" Elizabeth leaned forward, her heart thumping in anxiety. "And Mr. McNally? He's all right, isn't he?"

George shook his head. "I'm afraid he bought it, too, m'm. I'm right sorry to have to tell you this, but I thought you'd want to know."

Elizabeth sat back, stunned by the news. That energetic Scotsman, so full of life and vigor, gone. Just like that. She just couldn't believe it.

"Your ladyship?" Sadie placed a cup and saucer in front of her. "Drink this. I put a shot of brandy in it."

"Thank you, Sadie." Elizabeth reached for the cup, her hand unsteady, and Sadie moved around the table to pat Martin's shoulder with an unusual show of concern.

"Are you all right, me old luv? Drink your tea, then, there's a good boy."

For once, Martin showed no offense at being spoken to in such a familiar manner. Obediently he picked up his cup and brought it shakily to his lips.

"He's a bit upset, m'm," Sadie explained unnecessarily. "He thinks he's in a bomb shelter and that the manor's been bombed."

"I knew it would happen," Martin said, his voice wobbling. "I told everyone they'd drop those dratted bombs on us one day."

George gave him a pitying look. "They only bombed the factory, Martin, that's all. They've gone now, haven't they. That was all they was after. The factory. Now that's gone, they won't bother us again."

"Douglas McNally," Elizabeth said, putting down the cup. "I still can't believe it." She'd taken a hefty sip of tea and the brandy was still stinging its way down her throat. "We'll have to let his family in Scotland know. Did he have a wife? Children?"

"Not as far as we know, but we'll be looking into it." George drained his cup. "If you'll pardon me, m'm, I'd best be getting off. I'll have to be up early in the morning. The head office will be wanting a full report."

"Yes, of course." Elizabeth got slowly to her feet. "Thank you for letting us know. I'll stop by in the morning to see if there's anything I can do."

"Appreciate that, your ladyship." George pulled on his policeman's helmet and straightened it. "Not that there's much any of us can do for the poor buggers now, though."

"I suppose not. Goodnight, George."

Martin was still in the process of struggling to his feet

once more. Elizabeth reached across the table and took hold of the gun. He showed no resistance as she gently drew it out of his hand. Alarmed by the old gentleman's pallor, she motioned to Violet. "We must get him back to bed at once. All this has been a great shock to him."

"To all of us," Violet muttered as she hurried to take Martin's arm. "God help us all. Give us a hand, Sadie. Look sharp about it."

Sadie tossed the remains of her tea down her throat and smacked her lips. "It was worth getting up in the middle of the night for that," she said, putting her cup down on the table. "That's a good drop of brandy."

"For medicinal purposes, my girl, and don't you forget it." Violet glared at her. "Take hold of his other arm. It will take two of us to get him in bed."

Sadie hurried over to Martin's side. "Poor old bugger. Wonder what he'd do if we really did get bombed out of here. The shock'd kill him, I'm sure."

"Bite your tongue, missy," Violet snapped. "We've got enough trouble without you dreaming up more."

The door closed behind the three of them, leaving Elizabeth alone in the kitchen with the dogs. She went over to them and, much to their delight, knelt down beside them. Wrapping her arms around their thick necks, she murmured, "Dear George and Gracie. I never thought the war would come to Sitting Marsh. But now that it has, I promise I won't let anything happen to either of you."

The dogs thanked her with a sloppy slap of their tongues on her cheeks.

"I miss him so," she whispered in Gracie's soft ear. "He would have been such a tower of strength at a time like this." Tears slid down her cheeks. She rarely cried, but now she let the tears fall. For Douglas McNally and the loved ones he'd left behind. For the unfortunate charlady, and her grieving family.

She didn't know Jessie Bandini personally, but she knew the name. The middle-aged woman had lived with her daughter and baby granddaughter in a caravan not far from the village. There were rumors that they were gypsies, cast out by their tribe because the child had no apparent father.

She cried for them all. And she cried for herself, for her broken heart, and her own personal loss, made all the harder because she could not share her sorrow with anyone. No one except her beloved dogs.

Elizabeth slept late the next morning, and when she entered the office Polly was already at her desk. She looked up, her eyes filled with worry when Elizabeth greeted her. "They bombed the factory last night, m'm," she said.

"Yes, I know."

Elizabeth was still wondering if she should mention the deaths when Polly blurted out, "When I heard two people were killed, I thought it might be Ray. He sometimes works late at the factory. But then Sadie said as how it was Mr. McNally and Jessie Bandini. It's just awful. What are we going to do if they come back to bomb us again? We'll all be killed. I knew they should never have put up that factory." Her voice ended on a wail and she burst into tears.

Hurrying over to her, Elizabeth said soothingly, "Polly, there's no reason for the Germans to come back now. They've got what they wanted. It's over." She was repeating George's sentiments, and she hoped fervently that he was right.

Polly nodded tearfully. "That's what Sadie said, and Violet. It's just the shock, that's all. Everything's going wrong, m'm. Everything. What with me dad off fighting the war, and Sam gone back to America, and Marlene driving an ambulance at the front." She looked up at Elizabeth, her eyes wide with fear. "What if Marlene gets bombed, too? I couldn't bear it. I really couldn't." The tears started falling again.

Elizabeth gave the girl's thin shoulders a hug. "Now, now, this won't do. We can't let the enemy get us down like this. Where's that British stiff upper lip? Everything's going to be all right, you'll see. The war will be over soon, and your father will be home, and Marlene, too. Meanwhile, you have a nice young man to take care of you, haven't you?"

To Elizabeth's relief, a reluctant smile tugged at Polly's mouth. "Yes, m'm. He's really nice. I'm going to see him tonight. I'm just glad he wasn't there in the factory when it was bombed."

"Well, I'm sure all this will be forgotten soon." Elizabeth went back to her desk. "Now, let's get started on this pile of letters. I promised George I'd stop by the police station this morning, and it's nearly lunch time already.

"Tell you what, m'm." Polly left her desk and came over to collect the letters. "I'll take care of these, and you go on down to the police station. If there's anything I'm not sure about I'll ask you about it later."

Elizabeth beamed at her assistant. "Thank you, Polly. You have no idea how comforting it is to know I have such an efficient secretary."

Polly's face warmed with pleasure. "I do my best, I'm sure."

"And it's a very good best at that." Confident that Polly's smile meant she was feeling better, Elizabeth left the girl to her task.

George was at the front desk when she entered the police station an hour later. As usual, his mouth was full of

Banbury cake from Bessie's Bake Shop, and he chewed frantically as he staggered to his feet.

"Good morning, George," Elizabeth said brightly. Giving him time to answer, she called out to his partner in the back room, "You as well, Sid!"

"Morning, your ladyship," Sid's voice echoed back from behind the half open door. "Bit of excitement here last night, I reckon."

Having choked down the remnants of his cake, George said hastily, "Have a seat, your ladyship. I was hoping you'd drop by. I've got some important news for you."

Elizabeth took the chair he'd indicated, hoping it wasn't more bad news. Right now the people of Sitting Marsh had enough to deal with. By now the news of the bombing would be all over the village, and she would have her work cut out over the next few days trying to calm their fears. She folded her hands in her lap and tried to sound composed when she asked, "All right, George, what is it? What's happened now?"

CHAPTER
❀ 4 ❀

George coughed, then put on his official face. "We got the report from the fire department, your ladyship. It weren't no bomb what set the fire at the factory last night, after all. It were someone on the ground what did it. Which accounts for the fact that no one heard any airplanes."

Elizabeth stared at him in dismay. "Someone deliberately set fire to the factory?"

It was George's turn to look startled. "Oh, no, m'm. Not deliberate, no. Dave, the chief fireman, said it were an accident. Someone chucked a lit cigarette in a bucket of rags. Must have smoldered all evening and then caught fire. Course, once it reached the ammo, up it went."

"Oh, my." Elizabeth clutched her throat. "That must

have been quite an explosion. I'm surprised the whole village didn't hear it."

"Well, luckily, most of the explosives are stacked behind the main building. Dave said there were just a few boxes of ammo in that part of the factory, otherwise it would have taken out Fred Shepperton's farmhouse along with it. I always said he was taking a chance letting them build that thing on his land. His wheatfields are right alongside it."

"I understand it was Fred Shepperton who raised the alarm," Elizabeth said.

"Yes, m'm. Rode his bicycle down to the Tudor Arms, he did. Doesn't have a telephone. He told me he didn't want one of them newfangled things ringing in his house all day and night." George sniffed. "As if that many people would be bothering to call him."

"I still can't believe Douglas McNally is dead. I was just talking to him a week ago." She caught her breath. "How very ironic."

George looked puzzled. "Beg your pardon, your ladyship?"

"Oh, I was just remembering something Mr. McNally said." Elizabeth frowned. "He told me someone had been pushing threatening letters through his letterbox. Something about meeting his Maker. It just seems strange that this should happen to him now. I don't suppose he happened to mention anything about them to you?"

"Letters? Not so I can recall. I didn't have much to say to the gentleman. He always seemed to be in a big hurry. I don't reckon he could have been that worried about them letters though, or he would have reported it."

McNally's words were now echoing clearly in Elizabeth's mind. *Someone out there wants rather desperately to*

*see me dead and buried. And I have not the slightest doubt
he means business.*

He'd certainly sounded concerned about them. She was
the one who'd made light of them. "The firemen are quite
sure that it was an accident?" she asked sharply.

"Quite sure." George picked up a sheaf of papers. "They
went over everything as best they could. Of course, the place
were in a bit of a mess, seeing as how it had been blown up,
set on fire, and water poured on it, but the official word is
that it were an accident."

"You mentioned the fire chief. David something . . . what
was his name?"

"Dave Meadows. He's only part time, of course. All of
them are, aren't they. Volunteers, every one of them. All
the real ones are off fighting the war. Dave owns a repair
shop for bicycles in North Horsham. Does a bit of tinker-
ing with motorcars as well, I believe."

How well, Elizabeth wondered, *would a part-time volunteer fire chief be able to conduct an official investigation?* It
wouldn't hurt to find out. Remembering McNally's letters
had made her uneasy. And now that her mind was working
on the possibility of arson, there was something else bothering her. If only she could remember what it was.

"I have called this meeting," Rita Crumm's shrill voice an-
nounced, "to organize an official petition to close the munitions factory for good."

Crowded into Rita's tiny front room, the members of
the Housewives League gazed at their leader with vårying
expressions on their faces, most conveying boredom.

"What do we want to go and do that for?" Marge Gunther demanded. "It's already closed down."

"That's as maybe." Rita wore her hair pinned back,

except for a bunch of curls on top of her head that wobbled back and forth whenever she was agitated. The curls bounced joyfully as Rita tossed her head. "But there's talk that they're going to make repairs and reopen it as soon as possible."

"Who told you that?" Marge demanded over a chorus of muttered exclamations from the rest of the group.

"Never mind who told me." Rita preened, obviously enjoying her importance. "I just know, that's all. So we need to draw up a petition. After what's happened down there, we shouldn't have any trouble convincing people that a place like that is a death trap."

Nellie Smith sat on the floor in the corner and gritted her teeth. She was dying to say something sarcastic, but she'd already been suspended once from the Housewives League for mouthing off at Rita, and these days she did her best to keep her thoughts to herself. But it was hard. Especially at times like this, when that silly old cow acted like she was the only one who knew anything.

Nellie sighed. She didn't know why she bothered coming back to the League. She wasn't even a housewife, her not having been married and all. She'd had boyfriends, plenty of them. But none she'd wanted to marry. Besides, most of the young ones were off fighting the war.

In any case, British blokes were too bossy. From what she'd seen, they treated their wives like blooming slaves, expecting you to wait on them hand and foot and never a thank you at that. As for the Yanks, all they wanted was a good time. Come the end of the war, they'd be off back to America, with never another thought for the girls they left behind. She'd seen that happen already. To Polly Barnett for one.

Nah, women were better off without men. Much better off. Bloody savages, that's what men were. No better than the ape men in the Stone Age. All they wanted a woman for was to cook their meals, clean their houses, wash their clothes, and satisfy them in bed. Well, here was one woman who wasn't going to fall into that trap.

Nellie stretched out her legs to ease the ache in her knees. That's why she came back to the League. Much as she hated Rita Crumm and her lording over everyone, she liked a lot of the ladies and they were good company. Women friends, that's what really counted. Women friends didn't let you down and make you feel worthless.

"Are you with us or not, Nellie Smith?"

Nellie started, realizing that several pairs of eyes were fixed on her face. " 'Course I am," she said stoutly. "Let's get rid of that rotten factory once and for all."

Having missed breakfast, Elizabeth was ravenous when she arrived back at the manor, and she made straight for the kitchen. Violet was busily whisking batter in a bowl, and frowned at her when she sat down at the table. "Where did you get to this morning?"

"I overslept, and I needed to go into town to talk to George about the fire last night."

"Well, you shouldn't go without your meals, Lizzie. Not good for you."

"I'll make up for it now. I'm starving."

"Well, I tell you." Violet waved a whisk at Elizabeth. "I know at least one person who'll be glad to see that factory burnt down."

"I don't think it's completely burnt down." Elizabeth reached into the glass bowl of walnuts on the kitchen counter. "Though I understand one end of it has been badly damaged."

"Well, they won't be able to work in it, that's for certain."

She took the bowl away from Elizabeth. "If you eat these now there won't be enough left for the cake."

Elizabeth brightened. "We're having cake?"

"No, we're not having cake. This is for the bake sale the Housewives League is putting on at the vicarage. They're going to auction off cakes, and the money's going for more knitting wool so they can knit some more socks and scarves for our troops in the trenches."

Although she refrained from saying so, Elizabeth hoped that Violet's inadequate baking had not become common knowledge in the village. If so, her cake would not be raising too much money. "Who did you mean when you said someone would be happy to see the factory burn down?"

Violet poured her batter into a baking tin and set the empty bowl on the table. "Jack Mitchum, that's who. He was really upset about his wife going to work there and leaving him all alone to run the butcher shop. He's short-handed as it is, with his butchers all been called up; and with Millie gone it would have been really hard for him. Now she won't be able to work there any more, so he'll have her back in the shop with him. That'll make him happy, I bet."

Elizabeth stared at her. "Did Jack tell you this?"

"No, Marge Gunther told me. You know what a gossip she is. Apparently Jack and Millie had a big row about it right there in the shop in front of the customers and all. Marge said Jack was furious. Even accused Millie of having a crush on Mr. McNally, but Millie stood up to him. Told him she was going to do what she pleased and there was nothing he could do about it." Violet opened the oven door, letting out a blast of heat. "Good for her, that's what I say." She slid the pan of batter into the oven and shut the door. "There. That should be done in an hour or so."

"I hope you didn't use my egg ration for that cake," Martin said from the doorway.

Elizabeth, deep in thought, jumped at his voice.

"If you must know, Mister Miser," Violet muttered, "I didn't use eggs. I used the wartime recipe for the cake."

Martin sniffed and shuffled into the room, closing the door behind him. "Then I shan't eat any of it."

"It's not for you, so there." Violet turned on the tap over the sink and rinsed her hands. "It's for the bake sale, so you won't get any anyway."

Martin clasped his hands together and gazed up at the ceiling. "Thank you, Lord," he murmured.

Violet huffed out her breath. "Keep that up and you won't get any lunch, neither."

Ignoring her, Martin shuffled over to the table. "Good afternoon, your ladyship. May I be permitted to join you?"

Well used to this little ritual, Elizabeth said absently, "By all means, Martin."

"Thank you, madam. Much obliged, I'm sure." With great deliberation, Martin seated himself at the table. "I was wondering, madam, what plans we have for tonight."

With effort, Elizabeth dragged her mind back to the immediate present. "Tonight?"

"Yes, madam. I assume we shall be seeking shelter, in the event the Germans may return to bomb us again."

"Oh, I'm sorry, Martin. I forgot you didn't know. There was no bomb. The fire and explosion at the factory was an accident." Or so the fire department was saying. Something slipped into Elizabeth's mind, but was gone again before she could grasp it.

Martin looked disappointed. "No bomb?"

"No, Martin. No bomb."

"You mean all that excitement last night was over nothing?"

"I'd hardly call it nothing. After all, two people died in that fire." She remembered again the shock she felt when George had told her Douglas McNally had died. His words came back so clearly.

She sat up straight and banged her fist on the table.

Martin rose an inch off his chair with a little shriek. "What the devil was that?"

Violet spun around from the sink and stared at her. "Lizzie? Are you all right?"

"I'm quite all right," Elizabeth assured them. "I've just remembered something, that's all. Something important." She glanced at the clock. "I won't have time to wait for lunch, Violet. I have to go to North Horsham this afternoon. I must leave right away." She started to get up from the table, forcing Martin to struggle to his feet.

Violet pushed her fists into her bony hips. "Elizabeth Hartleigh Compton! You know better than that. You've already missed one meal. The soup's about ready. You can at least sit down and eat it."

"I'm sorry, Violet. This won't wait. I'll be back as quickly as I can. I'll take one of those apples to eat on the way."

"You'll be ill if you don't eat," Violet grumbled, handing over an apple.

Elizabeth headed for the door. "I'll be back as soon as I can."

"You'd better be back before it gets dark," Violet reminded her. "You can't ride that motorcycle with lights after blackout, and you won't be able to see without them."

"That's why I need to go now." Elizabeth let the door swing closed behind her and hurried up the steps to the front door. It would take her the best part of an hour to get to North Horsham on her motorcycle. She would have to be back by half-past four to beat the blackout. That gave her plenty of time to find Dave Meadows and talk to him. It would have been far quicker to ring him on the telephone, but from past experience she'd found that she got more information from people when talking to them face to face. Watching a person's expressions often told her more than their words.

She couldn't imagine how she could have missed the significance of George's words last night. Then again, she'd been woken up from a deep sleep. Her mind had been hazy, and the shock of hearing the news of McNally's death had made everything else insignificant at the time.

But these particular words had stuck in the back of her mind. *Locked inside the office, they were.* It seemed an odd thing to her, that Douglas McNally would lock himself and the charlady inside his office. It could mean nothing, of course, but under the circumstances, it was enough to merit a conversation with the fire chief.

She dragged her reefer coat from its peg on the hallstand and thrust her arms into the sleeves. Peering into the mirror, she wound a bright red knitted scarf around her head and tucked the ends into her coat to secure it. She looked rather like a peasant, she reflected, but it was far too cold to wear a hat on a long ride. She could have done with a ride in Earl's Jeep.

That would have been just as cold, she reminded herself as she ran down the steps and into the courtyard. Except with Earl at her side, she probably wouldn't have noticed. Though it was just as well he wasn't there to see her bundled up like this. Not at all elegant. Drat the winter. How she longed for the sunshine and warmer weather.

Her nose felt like a lump of ice by the time she arrived in

North Horsham. It only took a couple of questions at the post office to find out the address of Dave Meadow's bicycle shop. Weaving her way in and out of the town's heavy traffic, she was thankful that she lived in a small village like Sitting Marsh. Having to deal with all these buses, motorcars, and lorries every day would make her a nervous wreck.

It didn't help to notice how many American Jeeps were on the road, either. Every time she saw one her stomach lurched, in spite of the fact she knew perfectly well that Earl would not be in any of them.

The bicycle shop sat at the end of a side street, much to Elizabeth's relief. She found a spot to park her motorcycle not too far from the shop, and it only took a few brisk steps to bring her to the front door.

A bell jangled loudly as she pushed the door open. An elderly gentleman with white hair and whiskers stood behind a bench at the rear of the shop. He looked up from the bicycle wheel he was working on and seemed surprised to see her. "Lady Elizabeth, isn't it? From the Manor House in Sitting Marsh?" He moved around the bench and came toward her. "Well, I must say this is a pleasant surprise. What brings you to my humble abode?"

Elizabeth smiled graciously. "Mr. Meadows, I presume?" She was used to strangers recognizing her. After all, her picture appeared in the newspapers often enough. She was, however, surprised that the young, virile fire chief she'd imagined should turn out to be quite so advanced in his age. Then again, had he been young and virile, he would probably be overseas fighting for his country.

"You presume correctly, your ladyship. What can I do for you? A problem with your bicycle?"

"Actually it's a motorcycle," Elizabeth informed him, rather enjoying the way his eyebrows shot up in surprise.

"But no, there's nothing wrong with it, thank you. I wanted to talk to you about the fire last night at the munitions factory. I understand you were in charge of operations."

"That I was." Meadows pulled a chair out from behind the long counter and gestured for her to sit. "Quite a mess that was. The flames had taken a good hold by the time we got there. Luckily McNally had the foresight to install water pumps, and it didn't take us too long to put out the fire."

"The constables tell me there was an explosion." Elizabeth sat down and pulled off her fur gloves.

"A few rounds of ammunition, that was about it. According to the people we talked to this morning, there wasn't much in the way of explosives lying around. McNally did his job when it came to safety precautions. Poor devil. Never knew what hit him, I reckon. Or that poor old charwoman for that matter."

"Everyone thought it was a bomb at first."

"Well, you can thank the night watchman for that." Meadows shook his head in disgust. "Swore he heard airplanes overhead right after the explosion. He was so sure it was a bomb. It wasn't until we got word from the military that no airplanes had been sighted in the area that we started looking for the real cause."

"So you know exactly what started the fire?"

"Well, we've got a pretty good idea. There was a bin of oily rags sitting underneath an open window all afternoon, waiting to be picked up by the dustmen. We think someone was smoking outside and tossed the cigarette away without putting it out. That strong wind we had yesterday must have sent it through the window without anyone noticing. Looks like it landed in the rags, smoldered all evening, and around midnight, boom! Up she went."

"Isn't it odd," Elizabeth said slowly, "to have a window open on a cold winter's day?"

Dave Meadows shrugged. "A young chap told me it was opened to let out the smell of the rags. He also told me several people were outside smoking that afternoon, since they weren't allowed to smoke inside the factory. It could have been anyone who tossed that cigarette in the window."

"And you have no reason to suspect it could have been done deliberately?"

Meadows pursed his lips and gave her an odd stare. "What makes you say that?"

Elizabeth stroked the fur backs of her gloves. "It was just something George said when he was telling us about the tragedy."

"Oh, yes, P.C. Dalrymple. I talked to him this morning. Bit of a pompous ass, if you don't mind me saying so."

Elizabeth smiled. "He's not very happy about being dragged out of retirement. He's rather grudging about his job, I'm afraid."

"Well, I can understand that." Dave Meadows passed a hand over his forehead. "I'm not too partial to losing sleep either, but someone has to do the job. Good thing we don't get much in the way of bombs, or I'd be running all day and night. Not too many men left to volunteer for the fire department."

"I suppose not." Elizabeth paused. "Who found the bodies?"

"That was me. I was first inside the building. I had to break down the door to get to them. Saw them through the glass window, but I knew they were goners before I got to them."

"I see." Elizabeth got to her feet. "You said you had to break open the door?"

Meadows narrowed his eyes. "Pardon me asking, your ladyship, but why all the questions? I already sent in my report, and I don't think I left anything out."

Elizabeth smiled. "I'm sure you didn't, Mr. Meadows. It's just that I seem to remember George saying that the two victims were locked inside the office."

"That's right. It's there in the report, just like it happened."

"So I assume there was no key in the lock."

"I didn't see any keys, no, m'm."

"Doesn't it seem strange to you that Mr. McNally would lock himself and a charlady inside an office?"

The expression in his eyes grew harder. Obviously Dave Meadows was a man who did not like his judgement challenged. "I can't rightly say why he would do that, your ladyship, but I'm sure he had a good reason. All I can tell you is that we found the bin of rags and concluded that the fire started there. The windows were closed and locked when everyone went home that evening. There were no signs of forced entry. After questioning some of the employees, we're satisfied with our findings. We have no reason whatsoever to suspect the fire was deliberate. I suggest you talk to your constable if you have any more questions."

Aware that she had outstayed her welcome, Elizabeth thanked him and left. He might be satisfied, she told herself, but she was far from convinced it was an accident. She needed more answers, and she knew just where to start.

CHAPTER
❧ 5 ❧

Half an hour later Elizabeth reached the end of Sandhill
Lane and parked her motorcycle. Already, dusk was creep-
ing across the ocean and would soon engulf the village of
Sitting Marsh. The recent scare would no doubt make the
Home Guard all the more diligent with the blackout curtains
this evening. Elizabeth had about an hour before she needed
to be back at the manor. Enough time to accomplish her task.

Wally Carbunkle took so long to open the door after her
knock that she was about to leave when he finally opened
it. He wore a dark red smoking jacket, which he hastily
buttoned up when he saw her. "Lady Elizabeth! What a
surprise. Come in, come in." He waved a hand at the room
behind him. "You'll have to excuse the mess. I was up all
night and didn't feel like doing any housework."

Elizabeth stepped inside the tiny front room and waited for him to close the door. A newspaper lay at the feet of an armchair, and a tray with soiled dishes and an empty beer mug sat on the rough oak dining room table, but otherwise the place looked as spic and span as usual. Being an ex-navy man, Captain Carbunkle kept a trim ship.

"I'm sorry to disturb you," she said, as Wally motioned her to sit. "I hope you weren't sleeping."

"Not at all." He waited for her to seat herself on a roomy leather armchair, then he sat down on a sturdy rocker. "I was reading. Damn good book."

She picked up the opened book from the arm of the chair. "*Mutiny on the Bounty.* I'm surprised you haven't read it before."

"I have. This is the third time. Gets better with every reading."

She smiled and put the book down. "Wally, tell me what happened last night."

He coughed, looked down at his feet clad in elegant leather slippers, then said gruffly, "What are they saying?"

Surprised, she said warily, "Who?"

"The fire department. I assume that's who you've been talking to about it. That arrogant blowhard Meadows—" He coughed again, covering his mouth with his hand. "Excuse me, your ladyship. That sort of slipped out."

"That's quite all right, Wally. I have been talking to him, yes. All he said was that you were under the impression you had heard airplanes overhead after the explosion."

Wally heaved a heavy sigh. "I thought I did. Maybe I dreamt it." He gave her a sheepish look. "I have to admit, I fell asleep. Takes some getting used to, this working all night. I still haven't got turned around yet. I struggle to stay awake all night, then can't sleep in the daylight. Used to do it all the time at sea, but I can't seem to get the hang of it on land." He rubbed his knees with both hands. "I must be getting old."

"It would be difficult for anyone to get used to such a drastic change," Elizabeth assured him. "I'm not here to pass judgment on you, Wally. I just need to know everything that happened last night, as far as you can remember."

Wally closed his eyes for a minute, one hand absently stroking his beard. Finally he said, "Well, I got there at my usual time, just before six o'clock. The last people were just leaving. I hung my coat up in the men's room and then started my rounds. About a quarter to twelve I went back to the canteen. There's a nice comfortable chair in there and I sat down for a five minute break with the newspaper. I must have dozed off, because the next thing I knew, the ground shook and a noise like none I'd ever heard before just about burst my eardrums."

"The canteen is at the opposite end of the building to where the fire started, is it not?"

Wally nodded. "That's right, m'm."

"So what did you do next?"

"Well, the old ears were ringing like crazy and I was a bit dazed at first. That's when I thought I heard the planes. I was sure we'd been bombed. Everything had gone dark, and it took me a while to find my way out of the building."

"Did you see any smoke or flames?"

"No, but I could smell it. It was getting in my throat, making me cough. I tell you, I was bloody glad to get out in the fresh air."

"Then what happened?"

"Well, I stood there for a few minutes. Gave me quite a start to see the flames coming out of the windows. But then the roof started caving in at one end, so I knew I'd have to get the fire brigade. I wasn't going back in there to ring them, so I started off for Shepperton's farmhouse. It's the closest house to the factory. I was about halfway there when Fred came along on his bicycle. Said he'd already been down to the Tudor Arms and called the fire brigade. So he gave me a lift on the handlebars of his bicycle and we went back to the factory to wait for them to get there."

Thinking of Douglas McNally, Elizabeth briefly closed her eyes. "Before all this happened," she said, "did you see anyone else in the building that evening? After everyone else had gone, I mean."

Wally seemed surprised by the question. "Only Jessie, the char. She'd just got there and was hanging up her coat when I went into the canteen. Oh, and I saw Mr. McNally, too. We had a nice chat." He shook his head. "Nasty business that. Good chap, McNally was. And poor old Jessie. Can't believe it."

"It is a tragedy," Elizabeth agreed. "I shall call on her daughter to pay my respects. Do you happen to know her name?"

"Odd name, she's got." Wally frowned, then clicked his fingers. "Zora, that's it. Zora Bandini. She's got a little one. Don't know her name. I do know there's no father." He coughed. "Well, I'm sure there is one, but he's not around, if you know what I mean."

"It's all right, Wally, I understand." Elizabeth's stomach suddenly growled, reminding her she'd eaten nothing but an apple all day. Hastily she stood up to leave. "Zora lives in a caravan, I believe?"

"Aye, that she does. Down by Salishay Point, in Jeremy Quimby's fallow field. He lets them stay there and she helps him on the farm. Jessie stayed with the child while Zora was working. I don't know what she'll do now."

"Well, I'll call on her and see if there's anything I can do."

"That's jolly decent of you, your ladyship. I'm sure Zora will appreciate that very much."

She wasn't quite sure what she could do to help; but the least she could do was look in on the poor woman. Right now, however, she had a more pressing objective. And that was to get food inside her stomach as soon as possible, before it embarrassed her any further.

Polly sat in the back row of the Rialto cinema in North Horsham and wished that Ray Muggins would put his arm around her instead of sitting there stuffing his face with chocolates. After all, they were supposed to be her chocolates. He'd given them to her when he'd met her off the bus, and she'd got really excited. It had been ages since she'd had chocolates.

Now that sweets were rationed, it took at least a month to save up enough coupons for chocolates, and she didn't have the will power to go that long. She spent her coupons instead on a stick of nougat, or a packet of jelly babies.

Her mouth had been watering ever since Ray had put the box in her hands. All she'd had was one measly chocolate, and that was a cream center, not the kind she liked with the toffee in the middle. Just as the film started, she'd offered the box to Ray. She'd expected him to take one and leave the rest for her. Instead of that, he'd grabbed the box out of her hands and was now shoving a fifth chocolate in his mouth. She'd counted every one.

Not only that, she'd missed the beginning of the film because she'd been watching him. She hated missing the beginning of the film. It meant she'd be spending half the time trying to catch up on what happened.

She heard the rustle of the little paper cups as Ray reached for yet another chocolate. Cross with him now, she reached over and the took the box out of his hands. " 'Ere," she whispered fiercely. "Leave some for me."

"What?" He stared at her, his eyes wide and staring, like he'd seen a ghost. "Oh, sorry. I always eat too much when I'm bothered about something."

Come to think of it, he'd been acting funny all night. She wanted to ask him what was bothering him, but it was hard to talk in whispers. Instead she muttered, "I'll say you do." She looked down at the half-empty box. "You must have spent a month's coupons on these and they're nearly all gone already."

He shrugged. "Plenty more where they came from."

Not catching on, she demanded, "How can you? They're on coupons."

"Not where I get them."

She hissed out her breath. "You got them on the black market?"

He shushed her with a finger in front of his mouth. "Don't make such a big fuss about it, then. Everybody does it."

She didn't like being shushed like that. For a moment she thought about telling him so, but decided it wasn't worth arguing about. After all, he was right. Everybody did do it. It was the only way to get the things you liked, even if it did cost a lot more. Might as well enjoy them while she could. Snuggling down in her seat, she popped a chocolate in her mouth and started concentrating on the film. She had a lot to catch up on.

Elizabeth made sure she had a full bowl of porridge before she went up to the office the next morning. All night long she'd had strange, mixed-up dreams, most of which had included Earl. Not that she could really remember any of them very well, but she was quite sure they involved some activities she had no business allowing into her imagination, even if she wasn't in total control of her dreams.

Her face still felt warm at the thought as she entered the office. The first thing she saw was Polly's rear end stuck up in the air and her head hidden under her desk. Intrigued, Elizabeth murmured, "If you find anything interesting under there, do let me know."

A loud gasp was followed by a sharp crack as Polly's head hit the desk. Eyes streaming, her red face emerged over the side of the desk. "Good morning, your ladyship. You made me jump. I was just looking for me pencil. It must have rolled under the desk."

"I'm sorry I startled you." Elizabeth crossed the room to her own desk. "I hope you didn't hurt your head."

Struggling up into her chair, Polly rubbed the back of her head. "Not too bad. I needed something to wake me up this morning. I didn't get home until late last night, and me ma kept me up screaming at me for being late."

"I see." Elizabeth picked up a letter from the top of the pile and slit it open. "Out with your young man last night?"

"Yes, m'm. We went to the flicks. It was a very good film. It was called *The Shop Around the Corner,* and Jimmy Stewart was in it. It was about two people writing letters to each other and they didn't know they were writing to each other until the end of the film."

Elizabeth blinked. "I see. It sounds very . . . interesting."

"Oh, it were, m'm." Polly opened the drawer of her desk and started hunting in it. "It would've been a lovely evening if it hadn't been for the chocolates."

"Chocolates?"

"Yes, m'm. See, Ray bought me a box of chocolates, but he ate most of them 'cause he was so upset about Mr. McNally dying."

Elizabeth caught her breath. "Oh, that's right. I forgot your young man worked with Mr. McNally."

Polly looked up from her rummaging. "Yes, he did. He said as how Mr. McNally was the best boss he ever had and he was really, really upset when he found out he were dead. He said that Mr. McNally was like a father to him. See, Ray lost his dad in the first year of the war, and he really looked up to Mr. McNally. He sort of replaced his father, I s'pose." She uttered a little cry of satisfaction as she pulled a pencil out of the drawer. "I knew I had another one in here."

"How awful," Elizabeth said, feeling sorry for the young man. "It must have been a great shock to him to hear such dreadful news."

"Yes, m'm. It were. I never saw a bloke so upset. He actually had tears in his eyes when he told me. Gave me a right turn it did. I never saw a grownup bloke cry before. Not unless it were in a film, anyhow."

Elizabeth was beginning to feel better about Ray Muggins. At first she'd worried that he might not be good for Polly. City men were so much more devious and a good deal bolder than the village's young men. Hearing Polly speak about him that way, he sounded as if he was a sensitive and caring young man. Just what Polly needed after her unfortunate relationship with the American squadron leader, Sam Cutter.

"Ray was at the fire the other night," Polly was saying. "Saw the roof cave in, he did. Never thought for one minute Mr. McNally might be inside. It wasn't until the firemen brought out the bodies that Ray found out his boss were dead. Said it made him feel so bad he couldn't ride his bicycle back to the pub. So he walked all the way back and then had to go back and fetch his bicycle yesterday morning."

"Oh, dear." Remembering how shocked she'd been to hear of the tragic deaths, Elizabeth could sympathize with the young man. Losing his father must have been hard. She still hadn't fully recovered from losing both her parents so suddenly. Now the poor boy had lost a father figure in his life. So sad.

"Anyway, I reckon it's up to me to try and make him forget his troubles," Polly said, sounding so grown up Elizabeth had to smile.

"I'm sure you'll do a wonderful job," she told her assistant. "And when your young man is feeling better, I'd like to talk to him about what he saw the night of the fire."

Polly looked worried. "He doesn't like to talk about it, so he might not tell you very much."

"That's all right. I won't pressure him. I'd just like to know if he saw something that might help . . ." She broke off, aware that Polly was looking at her rather intently. She hadn't intended to voice her suspicions that the fire had been deliberately set. Then again, it would be only a matter of time before word got around. The village grapevine was more active than bees in a bed of roses.

"Ray said the fire was an accident," Polly said, looking uncertain. "He said as how the firemen said someone's cigarette fell in a bin of rags. They asked him lots of questions about it."

So Ray Muggins was the young man Dave Meadows had mentioned, Elizabeth realized. "Well, there's no reason to think otherwise at this point."

"But you think someone might have done it on purpose."

There was a tinge of fear in Polly's voice. Elizabeth hurried to reassure her. "Not at all. I just want to get everything straight, that's all. The fire chief seemed to be going on a lot of assumptions, and I thought I owed it to Mr. McNally to find out exactly what happened if I could."

It sounded lame, even to her ears, but at this point Elizabeth was not about to admit her doubts. For one thing, if someone was guilty of arson, it wouldn't do to alert him that she was on his trail. Better to let him, or her, think he got away with it.

"You think it was the three musketeers?"

Elizabeth frowned. She had to admit, that hadn't occurred to her. The musketeers were a band of mischief makers, possibly from an airbase near London, who seemed intent on causing as much grief as possible to the American airmen based near the village. So far the miscreants had been accused of everything from preventing the local farmers' chickens from laying to spoiling the milk at the Adelaide's dairy farm to poisoning several American airmen.

It had turned out that the musketeers had been guilty of none of these catastrophes. Nevertheless, they were responsible for damaging American Jeeps, causing accidents on the road, and generally making themselves a thoroughly unpleasant menace. It was only a matter of time before they became more reckless and caused more serious damage. Perhaps this was one of those times.

Elizabeth glanced at the clock. "I think I will take a run down into the village. I shan't be long. Perhaps you can take a look at these bills for me and sort out which are the most important. As usual, we won't be able to pay them all this month."

"I'll be happy to." Polly jumped up and gathered up the letters from Elizabeth's desk. "Better be careful, though, going down that hill. It's turned bitter cold out there again. There was ice on the road this morning when I came up on me bicycle. All the way up the driveway, too. And on the front step."

"I'll be careful," Elizabeth promised, touched by the young girl's concern.

Polly nodded, then said awkwardly, "I hope I didn't say nothing out of place just now. About the fire, I mean. I wouldn't want to get no one in trouble."

Elizabeth smiled. "Don't worry, Polly. I'm sure the firemen are right and it was all just an unfortunate accident." At least she would have been sure, she told herself as she hurried down the steps to the front hallway, if it hadn't been for that locked office door.

George seemed surprised to see her when she walked into the police station a little later. "I was just thinking about you, your ladyship," he told her, as she sat down on the visitor's chair. "I have some news that will please you, I do believe."

Elizabeth tugged off her fur gloves. "You've found out who set the fire at the factory?"

George's smile vanished. "Pardon me for saying so, but I've already told you the fire was an accident. I do hope and pray you're not going to make this out to be more than it is. We have enough trouble on our hands without going looking for more."

Elizabeth sighed. "George, have you ever known me to make trouble where none exists?"

"No, m'm, but I know how you are."

What exactly did that mean, Elizabeth wondered. Deciding that particular question could wait, she said firmly, "I'm as anxious as you are not to raise unnecessary fears in the residents of Sitting Marsh. I do, however, feel it my duty to assure them that a crime has not been committed. After all, two people have died under suspicious circumstances."

George's bushy eyebrows shot up. "Suspicious?"

Elizabeth leaned forward. "The door, George. The office door. It was locked. Mr. Meadows didn't seem to think that was at all odd, but in my opinion, it seems very odd for Mr. McNally to lock himself inside an office while the charlady is cleaning it."

George took a great deal of time shuffling papers around on his desk. He actually looked embarrassed, enough for Elizabeth to demand sharply, "George? Is there something you're not telling me?"

The constable shrugged and, avoiding her gaze, muttered, "I was only thinking; maybe McNally was engaged in a bit of hanky panky with Jessie. She was a good-looking woman. And you know what they say about gypsies."

Elizabeth didn't. Nor did she want to know. "That's nonsense. Douglas McNally didn't strike me as the sort of man who would engage in such nefarious conduct."

"What did Dave Meadows say about it?"

She clasped her hands together and straightened her back. "I have to tell you, George, I was not impressed with the man. He kept insisting that there was no need to suspect arson, and yet his conclusions were all drawn on conjecture. His speech was peppered with the words 'think' and 'perhaps.'"

"Beg your pardon, m'm, but I suppose that was the best he could do since the place was in such a mess."

"Yes, well, I was wondering if perhaps our nasty little musketeers had anything to do with that."

George's eyebrows twitched again. "Why would you think that?"

"They seem to have been the cause of a lot of trouble in the village over the past few months."

"Like I keep telling you, your ladyship, the fire at the munitions factory was an accident. Pure and simple. If the musketeers had anything to do with it they would have left their trademark. And nobody said nothing about letters being chalked on the walls or on the ground, and I can't see them going to all that trouble without letting people know they done it. They've always left three M's behind. Nope, as far as we're concerned, the fire chief's report is official. It were an accident. The case is closed."

"How long did it take the fire brigade to get to the factory, anyway?" Elizabeth demanded. "Is that in your report?"

Having apparently taken note of the irritation in her voice, George hastily shuffled through the papers on his desk again. "I don't see it here, your ladyship. I shall have to go through the files for it."

"It's right here," a voice piped up from the back office. Sid appeared in the doorway, looking a little disheveled, with what was left of his gray hair standing up on end. Sid had a bad habit of raking fingers through his hair when he got confused, which was nearly all the time. He held some papers, which he waved at Elizabeth.

George surged to his feet and snatched the papers from his partner's hand. "Thank you, Sid," he said, in a tone that suggested Sid would hear a good deal more about his intrusion later.

Sid grinned at Elizabeth. "Just wanted to help, that's all. That were some fire the other night, your ladyship. Lit up the whole sky, it did. Looked like Guy Fawkes Night, it did. If the Germans *had* been flying around, they would have seen it for miles."

"You saw it, Sid?" Elizabeth inquired. "Did you hear the explosion?"

Sid nodded with great enthusiasm. "I did, indeed, m'm. Woke me and the missus up, it did. I told her, soon as I heard it, that's something big, I said. I thought it were a bomb, until I got there and the firemen told me it were an accident. Quite a few people were enjoying the spectacle up there."

"Anyone you recognized?"

Sid opened his mouth to answer, when George rudely butted in. "Sid has some important business to take care of, don't you, Sid?"

Sid sent him a vacant look. "I do?"

"Yes, you do." George pointed a finger at the door. "In the back room. All those files have to be put away."

"Bloody office boy, that's all I am," Sid grumbled. "Join the police force, they said. Enjoy a life of adventure. Nobody said nothing about spending most of your time doing boring paperwork. All that filing and making out reports makes you crossed-eyed, I swear."

"Sid!"

George's roar made even Elizabeth jump.

"All right, I'm going." Sid nodded at Elizabeth. "Ta ta, your ladyship."

George rolled his eyes but Elizabeth nodded graciously. "Good morning, Sid."

"I'm sorry, your ladyship," George muttered, when Sid had disappeared. "He means well, but he's a little short on the old pistons, if you know what I mean."

"I heard that!" Sid called out from the back office.

"Anyway," George said hurriedly. "I wanted to tell you the good news. That quack in North Horsham what operated on the Adelaide girl . . . what was her name? Barbara?"

Elizabeth sat up. "Barbara, yes, that's it. You found him?"

George nodded with satisfaction. "That fiend will never operate on anyone else, I can promise you that."

"Thank God." The year before, Elizabeth had promised a bereaved mother that she would find the monster who had caused her daughter's death. Ever since then she had hounded George to track down the brute. She could still see Annie Adelaide's face when she was describing how her youngest daughter had an abortion and bled to death as a result of the botched efforts of a fake doctor. She nodded with satisfaction. "I hope the news will bring the Adelaides some peace."

"My sentiments exactly, m'm. They seemed pleased when I told them." George peered meaningfully at the clock on the wall. "Now, if you'll excuse me . . ."

"The report, George?" Determined not to be distracted from her purpose, Elizabeth pointed at the papers on his desk. "May I see it?"

George tightened his lips. "I'm afraid not, your ladyship. This is police business, and as such, shall remain private. The case is closed as far as we are concerned, and I sincerely hope you will let the matter rest."

Elizabeth got to her feet and pulled on her gloves. "I can't do that, George. Two people died in that fire, locked inside an office. Having seen the office myself, I know it has one of those locks that operates on both sides of the door. I'm not going to let anything rest until I know why Mr. McNally locked that door. And if he didn't lock it himself, that means someone else must have locked it from the outside. Which would mean, if I am right, that we have a particularly heinous murderer in our midst."

CHAPTER
❄ 6 ❄

One of the reasons she missed Earl so much, Elizabeth reflected as she coasted cautiously up the icy hill to the mansion, was that she had no one to talk things over with at the end of the day. So often she could sort things out in her mind after having spent an evening over cocktails in the refectory with Earl.

This was one of those times when she wished desperately he were there to share her concerns. Admittedly, she had only her own instincts to go on, but she couldn't ignore the feeling that everyone was missing something. Something important.

Maybe McNally did have a good reason to lock the door that night. After all, it was a munitions factory, making arms and ammunition to help destroy an enemy. Some of the information he had stored in his files had to be sensitive material and not for everyone's eyes. Especially a charlady, who might be inclined to spread the news of anything she might find out about such an important and controversial business.

But then, if the woman was already in his office, and he with her, why would he need to lock the door? According to Wally, they were the only two people in the building besides himself. It just didn't make sense.

She absolutely refused to believe that Douglas McNally was involved with his charlady. Then again, she might have been more ready to accept the fire was an accident, had it not been for the threatening letters Mr. McNally talked about.

Having reached the entrance to the Manor House driveway, Elizabeth cut down her speed. Cruising slowly up the avenue of trees, she sorted out in her mind what she already knew.

Wally had been woken up by the explosion and had barely escaped from the smoke-filled building. Fred Shepperton, less than half a mile away, had also woken up, got dressed, and rode his bicycle down to the Tudor Arms—about a ten minute ride—to alert the fire brigade. He'd then returned to find Wally on his way to the farm and had given him a ride back to the factory.

It would have taken the fire brigade at least thirty minutes to arrive at the factory, at which time they had broken down the door of the office and found the two bodies. The big question was, if McNally and Jessie had heard the explosion, which obviously they must have done, why hadn't they made any attempt to leave? *Because the door was locked from the outside?*

Elizabeth roared into the courtyard and cut the engine. No matter what the fire chief's report said, or what George believed, something was wrong with that whole picture. And, since nobody but her seemed concerned about that, it was reasonable to assume that she alone would have to solve the puzzle.

The first place to start, she decided, was with the threatening letters that Douglas McNally had received. Apparently, relatives would be arriving the next day to clean out the house he'd rented on the outskirts of the village. She'd managed to get that much out of George before she'd left. That meant if she was going to search the house for those letters, it would have to be that afternoon.

Elizabeth climbed off the motorcycle and wheeled it into the stables. McNally's house was not on her estate, which meant she had no official sanction to enter it. On the other hand, as guardian of the village and its people, she considered it her right—no, her *duty*—to go anywhere in order to preserve the safety and comfort of her tenants. If that meant breaking a few rules in order to apprehend a murderer, well, so be it.

Emerging from the stables, she noticed a Jeep standing empty in the courtyard. As always, her stomach turned over at the sight of it. She remembered vividly the first time she'd seen a Jeep parked outside the manor. It had been her first indication that her world was about to be turned upside down.

The orders from the war office requisitioning her home for the use of American officers had come as a dreadful shock. Even so, nothing had prepared her for her immediate attraction to the handsome major who had delivered the news.

Earl Monroe had impacted her soul as no other man had ever done. Standing so tall, his skin burned by the sun, his eyes as clear and blue as frosted glass, his hair streaked with gold, he'd brightened her somber library with a powerful image of endless skies and wide open plains.

When she'd learned that he was married, her disappointment had been far beyond the limits of protocol. Her breeding and her position in society had helped her fight the forbidden yearnings, but her heart had succumbed to the inevitable, and try as she might, she could not erase the memory of him from her mind.

He would always be hovering in the background, ready to spring back as formidable and enticing as ever, every time she saw something to remind her of him. As right now, with that empty Jeep parked almost in the very same spot as the day she'd first set eyes on him.

There were times, Elizabeth mused, as she climbed the steps to the front door, when she wished she'd never met him. Life was comparatively dull before that, but at least she had a measure of peace. It seemed now as if she were doomed to suffer the torment of missing him for the rest of her born days.

Deep down, however, she knew she wouldn't have missed those incredible months for anything. Earl Monroe had given her companionship, laughter, intense debates, and a tantalizing excitement that still haunted her when she thought about him. He had made her take a good look at herself, and what she discovered had surprised and pleased her. He had made her more alive, more aware. He'd made her understand her strengths and her weaknesses, and for that she would forever be grateful to him.

Elizabeth tugged the bell rope and listened to its chime deep in the hallway inside. Even if she had to bear the sadness of what might have been for the rest of her life, it was worth it to know such a man.

Deep in the inescapable memories, it was some time before she realized that no one seemed to be coming to open the door. Violet would be busy in the kitchen right now, preparing lunch. Sadie was probably in the east wing, cleaning the officers' lavatories. Polly was presumably still in the office and wouldn't hear the bell, either. Which left Martin, whose job it was to open the door, and who apparently had also failed to hear the bell.

Elizabeth tugged on it again, promising herself as she had so often to install a conventional lock on the front door instead of all the bolts and latches that had to be lifted from the inside to let someone in.

Again she waited, then, growing impatient, she hung determinedly on the bell rope. There must have been a sheen of frost left on the step—her feet slid out from under her. Still holding onto the rope, she swung around until her back was to the door, just as she heard the bolts being shot back.

Feeling ridiculous, she swayed back and forth, struggling to get back on her feet. To let go of the rope threatened to deposit her on her back, yet she couldn't seem to bring the rope close enough to her body to regain her balance.

The door creaked open behind her, just as she finally got a foothold on the slippery step. Cross that she was presenting a rather inelegant image to her butler, Elizabeth thrust the rope away from her, saying crossly, "Where have you been, Martin? It's freezing out here."

The voice that spoke behind her didn't belong to Martin, however. It was a voice she knew well. A deep, husky voice with the faint burr of the American West. A voice she thought she would never hear in her lifetime again.

"I was expecting a better welcome than that for a long lost friend."

In the act of turning around, Elizabeth froze. She was afraid to look, afraid she was imagining that beloved voice. Ridiculously, she said the only thing that popped her into her mind. "Martin?"

The soft chuckle set every nerve in her body tingling. "Come on, Elizabeth. Do I really sound like Martin?"

With a cry of joy she turned . . . and there he was. Looking just the same as the day she'd last seen him. No . . . more tired maybe. There were little lines of strain at the corners of his mouth. But oh, he was handsome. So incredibly virile. She tried to speak, but no words would come. Unashamed of the tears spilling down her cheeks, she thrust out her hands.

He seized them both in his, and even through the fur of her gloves she felt the warmth of his grasp. "It's so damn good to see you again," he said, pulling her inside.

He let her go to slide the bolts back in place. Still she couldn't speak. She just stared at him helplessly, still afraid she would blink her eyes and he would vanish back into the recesses of her fertile mind.

"I heard the bell ringing," Earl said, as he turned to her again. "No one seemed to be answering it, so I figured I'd better open the door before you gave up and left."

She cleared her throat. "You knew it was me?"

"I heard the motorbike. I'd been waiting to hear that sound for almost an hour."

"But how . . . when . . . ?"

"Let's go down to the conservatory and I'll tell you everything. Here, let's get you out of this." He reached for her scarf and unwound it from her head. Embarrassed, she pulled off her gloves, then tried to pat her ruffled hair back into place, but then he started unbuttoning her coat and she hurried to help him. As he pulled the coat from her shoulders she was terribly glad she'd worn her favorite blue fluffy twin set with her pleated skirt. Though she would have much preferred to be wearing something a little more glamorous for their reunion.

She watched him hang her coat on the hallstand, still unable to believe he was actually there in front of her. So many times she'd imagined seeing him again. So many times she'd played the images in her mind. Though somehow in her dreams it had always been summertime, and they'd met running toward each other on the cliffs. Not at all like this dreary winter day in her darkened hallway.

Not that she cared how they'd met again. She ached to touch him, to hug him, to convince herself he really was there in the flesh and not some wild vision conjured up by her longing.

He turned to her, and now she felt uncomfortable, remembering their last moments together. She'd watched him walk out of the conservatory, knowing that it was probably the last time she'd see him.

In that moment she'd wished with all her heart that she hadn't been quite so determined in her efforts to observe the principles of her upbringing and her heritage. He'd taken her by surprise when he'd suddenly returned to her side. His forbidden kiss had been brief, so long awaited, and so bittersweet. He'd left before she'd fully recovered.

Gazing now on his beloved face, she wondered if she'd ever recovered from that moment. All the old yearning, the ache of wanting what one couldn't have, returned in full force. Long-held scruples made her say abruptly, "How's your wife? Your son? I hope he's fully recovered from the car accident?"

A shadow crossed his face. "Brad's just fine. He's started his first year of college and seems to be doing very well."

"I'm glad to hear it. And your daughter?"

"Marcia's doing great. She's working for a small theater in Laramie."

"Laramie?"

"It's a city not far from where we live." He took a step toward her, then halted as she backed away from him.

"I . . ." she looked around, half hoping to see Martin shuffling toward them. She didn't want to be alone with Earl right now. She was too vulnerable. Too afraid she might not have the strength to resist temptation. "Would you like some tea?"

Aware how silly that sounded, she drew in a shaky breath. And then he said the last thing in the world she expected to hear.

"Elizabeth, I'm getting a divorce."

"I got a letter from Marlene yesterday," Polly said. She was at her desk in the office, watching Sadie's half-hearted efforts to dust the furniture.

Sadie grasped this opportunity to take a break. "Go on! What's she doing? Does she like driving an ambulance? Has she met a bloke out there yet?"

Polly laughed. "She's met lots of blokes. Only most of them are banged up from the fighting, aren't they."

Sadie pulled a face and flopped down on the rocking chair. Bouncing back and forth she muttered, "You know what I mean."

Polly's smile faded. "Yeah, I do. She doesn't mention anyone special. Just talks a lot about the wounded, and how hard it is to see them. She doesn't just drive the ambulance. She talks to the blokes, holds their hand, writes letters for them, all that stuff."

"Good for her." Sadie rocked harder. "It must be lovely to know you're doing something that important for the war effort."

Polly looked down at her blotting paper and started

drawing a house with her pencil. "Yeah, I s'pose so. I wish I could do something for the war effort."

Sadie stopped rocking. "Like what?"

"I dunno. Just something."

"Well, you're not old enough to drive an ambulance in Italy, if that's what you're thinking. Your ma would never let you go, anyhow."

"I know. I don't mean that." Polly dug her pencil harder into the blotting paper. "It's just that when I think of all them soldiers fighting and getting wounded and dying, I feel like I should be doing something for them."

"Well, you can. Why don't you join the Housewives League? They do all sorts of things for the war effort. You can knit socks and scarves for the soldiers, collect tinfoil, like the caps off the milk bottles and those little papers inside the cigarette packets. They're always doing something to raise money for the troops and making up parcels of food and stuff to send to them."

"Not on your life. I'm not going to muck around with a bunch of old geezers listening to clicking knitting needles. I have enough of that with me ma. Besides, I hate Rita Crumm."

Sadie laughed. "I don't blame you. Well, what about your victory garden? You work on that, don't you?"

Polly shuddered. "Not since I found a blinking dead body in it, I don't. Even ma don't like working in there now."

Sadie started rocking again, more gently this time, a frown of concentration on her face. After a moment, she snapped her fingers, making Polly jump. "I know what you can do!"

"What?" Polly looked at her warily, having heard too many of Sadie's outlandish ideas.

"You can write letters."

"What letters? Who to?"

"The soldiers, silly." Looking excited now, Sadie stopped rocking and leaned forward. "What's the one thing the soldiers look forward to more than anything?"

"The grub?"

Sadie snorted. " 'Course not. Don't you ever listen to the news on the wireless? No, it's letters from home. Lots of them don't even get letters. All you have to do is ask Marlene for the names and addresses of the blokes who don't get any, and you can write to them."

"I don't know—" Polly began doubtfully, but apparently caught up in her excitement, Sadie butted in.

"What's more, you can get others to write, too. I bet there's lots of women would be only too happy to write a letter now and then. Just think how happy you'd make those lonely soldiers out there, to know that back home there's a bunch of women who really do care what happens to them."

The more Polly thought about it, the more she started to like the idea. "We could put notices up in the village hall and in the post office. Paste 'em up all over the village. We can tell them to ask me for an address."

Sadie bounced up and down in excitement, making the rocker creak. "Yeah, yeah! This is a bloody marvelous idea, if I say so meself. I'll write to one of the blokes, even though I'm going out with Joe. I know he won't mind."

Polly dug the pencil so hard in the blotting paper the point snapped. "I'll write to Marlene tonight and ask her to send the addresses. Though it might take a while. It took her letter ages to get here."

"Never mind. We can spend the time lining up a bunch of people who want to write. And by the time we get the addresses, we'll have letters ready to go off right away. We'll just tell everyone to write a letter telling someone all about themselves, where they live, about their family, things they like, things that are happening in the village, and when we get the addresses, we'll send them all off. After that it will be up to the blokes if they write back."

Polly looked at her in awe. "Sadie, this really is a smashing idea. Let's get started on it tonight. We can go down to the pub and start asking people there. I bet Alfie will let us put up a notice in the pub, too."

Sadie got up from the chair, leaving it to rock gently back and forth by itself. "Can't. I'm going out with Joe tonight. But tomorrow, we'll do it. Besides, we have to make the posters first."

"Oh, right. I'll ask her ladyship for some paper. She has some big sheets of it she keeps for announcements." Polly caught her breath. "Wait! I can ask Ray to help me. He's clever with that sort of thing."

"Good idea." Sadie grinned. "Give you a good excuse to see him, won't it."

Polly tossed her head. "I don't need an excuse. He keeps asking me to go out with him."

"So why don't you go, then?"

"I don't know." Polly stuck a pencil sharpener on the end of her pencil and started twisting it. "I like him and everything, but . . ." She let her voice trail off, not knowing exactly how to finish that sentence.

"He's not Sam," Sadie finished for her.

"I'm over Sam." Polly pulled the sharpener off the pencil, spraying little bits of wood everywhere. "Besides, I went out with Ray the other night. I don't have to see him every night, do I?"

"All right, all right! Don't get your knickers in a twist." Sadie moved toward the door. "If you can get at least one poster ready by tomorrow, we'll go down the pub tomorrow night, all right?"

Her irritation vanishing, Polly sent her a cheerful wave. "I'll have one ready. I'm really looking forward to this. I feel like I'm doing something to help, even if it's not as important as what Marlene is doing."

Sadie peered back at her through the half-closed door. "Any time we can put a smile on a lonely soldier's face, I'd say that's every bit as important as driving an ambulance. Ta ta for now!"

Polly stared at the closed door for a moment, then smiled. Sadie was right. If they could gets lots of people writing letters, that would be really important. She reached for a sheet of paper and then dipped her pen into the inkwell.

Slowly she began writing. *Dear Soldier, my name is Polly Barnett and I live in a village called Sitting Marsh. . . .*

Elizabeth stared at Earl, trying to understand exactly what he was saying. She kept hoping he'd say something else, but he seemed to be waiting for her answer to this stupendous bit of news.

The long silence was abruptly broken by Martin's quavering voice. "Oh, there you are, madam. I thought I heard the bell. Unfortunately I was . . . ah . . . indisposed at the time. I deeply apologize for keeping you waiting."

"That's all right, Martin," Elizabeth murmured, her gaze still locked with Earl's. "The major let me in."

The sound of shuffling feet drew closer. "The major? 'Pon my soul! So it is." Martin came into view, his forehead deeply creased as he peered at Earl over the top of his glasses. "I thought we'd seen the last of you."

This rather rude observation broke the tension as Earl

laughed. "Can't get rid of me that easy, Martin. How are you? Long time, no see."

"Is the war over, then?" Martin looked at Elizabeth. "I'm sure we would have heard if there had been a victory, madam, don't you think?"

"I'm afraid the war is still going on," Elizabeth told him.

"Then what's he doing here?" Martin jerked his head in Earl's direction.

Embarrassed, Elizabeth glanced at Earl's amused face. "I was rather wondering that myself."

"I've been reassigned here for a while." Earl held out his hand to Martin. "I hope that meets with your approval, Martin?"

Martin regarded the proffered hand with suspicion, then shakily held out his gnarled fingers. "Good to see you again, young fellow. Things have not been the same around here since you left." He shook Earl's hand, then to Elizabeth's further embarrassment, gave her a sly wink. "I trust that your disposition will improve now, madam?"

"My disposition is in very good health, thank you, Martin," Elizabeth assured him crisply. Actually, that was putting it mildly. At that moment she was having a great deal of trouble resisting the urge to leap about madly with ear-splitting shrieks of joy. "Major Monroe and I will be taking lunch in the conservatory. Will you please ask Violet to prepare a tray for us?"

"Of course, madam." Martin shuffled away at his usual snail's pace. "Right away."

"I'm sorry," Elizabeth murmured as he disappeared. "I'm afraid Martin tends to speak rather bluntly at times."

"It's good to see him again." He smiled at her, his eyes

crinkling at the edges as she remembered so well. "It's good to see you, too, Elizabeth."

"Likewise." She felt tongue-tied, like a schoolgirl again. Part of her was bubbling over with joy and excitement, yet she was afraid to rejoice too much. She was terrified that she'd misunderstood him, even more terrified of what it might mean if she'd heard him right. She felt as if she'd been caught up in a whirlwind, head spinning, feet off the ground.

He held out his arm, and his eyes were full of warmth and sparkle as he murmured, "Shall we?"

She placed her hand in the crook of his elbow. She'd worry about everything later. Right now she was living what she'd thought was a hopeless dream, and she was going to enjoy it for all it was worth before the bubble burst once again.

CHAPTER
❧ 7 ❧

It was much later before Elizabeth was alone with Earl. When they arrived at the conservatory, the first thing he commented on was the absence of his favorite rocking chair. Rather than wait to find Desmond and ask him to fetch it from the office, he suggested going up to get it himself.

Elizabeth went with him, and several minutes were taken up talking to Polly, who seemed delighted to see the major again. Eagerly she plied him with questions about America, until Elizabeth had to drag him and the chair from the room.

Between them they carried the heavy rocker all the way down the stairs, stopping every now and again to catch their breath. With all the laughing and joking together, Elizabeth couldn't help noticing how much more at ease Earl had become.

In spite of the lines of strain she'd noticed earlier, he seemed more light-hearted, more boyish than she'd ever seen him. It made him all the more attractive, and by the time they got the chair situated just right and Earl had sunk onto it with a long sigh of satisfaction, Elizabeth had serious doubts about her ability to refrain from flinging herself into his arms and begging him to repeat the kiss he'd given her a lifetime ago.

Seated on the wicker couch, she accepted the glass of sherry he'd poured for her and tried not to notice the visible trembling of her hand. Aware that Violet would appear at any minute with their meal, she was determined to get one thing straight before she died from apprehension.

"How long will you be staying this time?"

"I don't know." He settled his broad shoulders against the back of the chair, tilting it backward. "I asked for the transfer and they gave it to me, but on a temporary basis. Though I'm gonna work on that."

"Will you be moving back into the manor?"

It disturbed her to see the odd look in his eyes. "If you'll have me."

"Of course we'll have you! Violet will be delighted, I'm sure, and even Martin has missed you, in spite of what he says."

"Then I'll move in tonight."

"What about Major Barnes? Didn't he replace you?"

"He's been reassigned. Somewhere near London, I think."

"Your men will be pleased to hear that." Not nearly as thrilled as she was, she reflected happily.

The look in his eyes intensified. "I've missed you, Elizabeth."

"I've missed you, too." This was dangerous ground, she

warned herself. Her heart was thumping so hard she was sure he could hear it. Better watch every word she said, or she might say something she'd regret later on.

To her disappointment, he seemed satisfied with that. "So tell me what's been happening in Sitting Marsh. I hear you had a some excitement here the other night."

She didn't want to talk about the fire at the factory. She wanted to talk about the stunning statement he'd made earlier. She wanted to know if he'd really said those words or if she'd imagined the whole thing. She wanted to know, if it were true, what it would mean to their relationship.

All the hoping, wishing, and wanting she'd suffered through now seemed immoral, as if her intense longing for him had somehow engineered this state of affairs. She'd ached to hear those words ever since he'd told her his marriage wasn't all it should be, and now that he'd actually said them, she wasn't sure how she felt.

"Elizabeth?"

Mortified, she realized she'd been staring at him for several moments without speaking. "I'm sorry," she said quickly. "I'm afraid my mind was on something else just then."

"You're thinking about what I said earlier, about the divorce."

He always could read her mind so well. "Yes," she said, clasping her hands together to disguise their trembling, "I was—"

To her dismay, a tap on the door interrupted her. Violet pushed her way in, carrying a loaded tray.

Earl leapt to his feet to take the tray from her, earning himself a rare smile from the cantankerous housekeeper. "How's my favorite girl?" he asked, as he set the tray down on the low table.

"Oh, go on with you, Major," the housekeeper simpered. I bet you tell all the girls that."

Elizabeth was intrigued to see Violet's cheeks grow warm. She inspected the tray, pleased to see the tempting array of cheeses, pork pie, sliced apples, and thick crusty bread. Violet must have squandered a month's rations. "Thank you, Violet," she murmured. "You've outdone yourself."

"Can't do too much for the major," Violet said, beaming at Earl. "It's nice to see you back."

"It's good to be back, Violet. I've missed living at the manor. My house in the States seemed a little cramped after this."

"I bet you don't miss the rattle in the water pipes." Violet sent a sly glance at Elizabeth. "Or the ghosts."

"I missed everything about being here. Especially the dogs. Where are they, anyway?"

"Asleep in the kitchen. They don't move much in this cold weather. Drafty old place this is."

Violet showed no sign of leaving, much to Elizabeth's frustration. She couldn't wait for the housekeeper to leave so she could finish her vitally important conversation with Earl. "This looks very good," she said, giving Violet a meaningful look. "You must be starving, Earl."

"As a matter of fact I am."

"Well, I'd best be off and let you enjoy your meal." Violet finally moved, all too slowly in Elizabeth's opinion, to the door.

The second it closed, she turned back to Earl. "I'm sorry, I—"

"Wait." He sat down on the rocker again, his hands thrust between his knees. "I've been thinking about this all the way across the Atlantic, rehearsing what I wanted to say to you when I saw you. So let me speak, and if you have any questions after that I'll do my best to answer them, okay?"

Heart pounding, she whispered, "All right."

"Well, as I said, my wife and I are getting a divorce. It had nothing to do with any situation here. This had been brewing for some time. In fact, it was my wife who asked for the divorce. Although she didn't say as much, I have an idea she wants to be free to meet someone else."

Elizabeth uttered a small cry of distress. "I'm so dreadfully sorry."

His smile was a little guarded. "Don't be. As I said, it came as no real surprise. In fact, it was a relief. Because now I'll be free to follow a different path."

If she hadn't had such difficulty breathing, she would have answered him, though she had no idea what she would say. It didn't matter, anyway, because Earl went on talking.

"The divorce won't be final for a few months yet. Knowing how you feel about protocol and image and all that, I'll keep my distance until I'm officially free. After that, I guess I'll find out how you really feel about me."

As if he didn't know. Everyone else in the manor knew how she felt about him. He had to know. The fact that he was willing to wait in respect of her position before declaring himself only deepened her feelings for him. And yet, now that the impossible had suddenly become a very real probability, all sorts of warning bells were ringing in her head.

How open could they be about their relationship? She was the lady of the manor, revered and respected by her tenants. In spite of her own divorce, she'd earned their trust. They looked upon her as the one reliable constant in a rapidly changing world.

They expected a certain criteria of behavior from their guardian, and anything less would destroy their faith and conviction that life would go back to normal once the war was over. That was what kept these people going—allowed them to go on living their lives—the powerful belief that things would be as they once were.

Even if they could accept a divorced woman in love with a divorced man as someone to look up to, what future could there possibly be for them? Sooner or later, he would have to return to America. If she wanted a lasting relationship with him, she'd have to follow him there.

How could she leave her home, this village, without leaving an heir to take her place? And what would happen to Violet and Martin? What would they do without her?

"I know I said I'd keep my distance," Earl said, breaking in to her thoughts, "but I was hoping for an indication that you felt at least some pleasure at the news."

Putting her worries aside for now, she smiled at him. "If the divorce is what you want, then of course I'm delighted. I'd be lying if I said I wasn't. It just seems so . . ."

"Seems so what?"

"It just seems dishonorable to rejoice over the end of a marriage."

He squinted his eyes, as if trying to see inside her mind. "How did you feel when your marriage ended?"

"Relieved," she admitted. "It was a miserable marriage, anyway. The divorce was uncivilized, and it was a great load off my shoulders to have it over."

"Well, at least my divorce was amicable. We're still friends. Just grown apart, that's all. But that's exactly how I feel. Relieved. I don't think there's any shame in celebrating that, do you?"

"Perhaps not." She picked up her sherry glass. "Here's to your return to Sitting Marsh. I hope you will enjoy it as much as I shall."

"I certainly intend to do my best." He raised his own glass, clinked it against hers, then took a sip. "Now, let's eat. Then you can tell me what's been going on in Sitting Marsh."

They began to eat the tasty meal and she told him about the opening of the factory, and the fire. She watched his face grow grave when she told him that she was convinced the fire had been set on purpose, and that she suspected Douglas McNally and Jessie either died before the explosion or were unable to escape from the office.

"Are you sure someone was out to murder McNally?" Earl asked, helping himself to a large slice of the cold pork pie.

"Well, you have to admit, the locked door does raise some valid questions."

"I guess. Are there any suspects?"

"Not yet." Elizabeth crunched on a juicy slice of apple. "I've only just arrived at the conclusion that it wasn't an accident. I think it's likely that whoever wrote those threatening letters to Mr. McNally is responsible, so I need to find out who that person is."

"What do the constables say about all this?"

"According to the fire chief's report, the fire was caused by a cigarette accidentally thrown into a bucket of oily rags. George is sticking with that and refuses to listen to any theories I might have. I think he just doesn't want to be bothered with an investigation unless he's forced into it."

"Sounds familiar."

Elizabeth sighed. "To be honest, I'd just as soon look into it myself. That way I won't be treading on any toes."

"The problem with that," Earl said, leaning back in his chair, "is that it usually lands you in trouble."

"I know." She smiled at him. "But now that you're back,

I don't have to worry about that. If I do run into a problem, I'm quite sure you'll be there to rescue me."

He didn't answer her smile. "You can't be sure about that. It's not as if I'm around all the time. Sometimes it'll be days before we'll see each other."

She leaned forward and patted his hand. "Don't worry, Earl. I'll be careful."

Before she could withdraw her hand, he turned his up and grasped her fingers. "You'd better promise me that. I didn't come all the way back here to Sitting Marsh to see something bad happen to you."

Yes, she thought, with a little rush of anticipation, *things had changed between us.* It was subtle, but there, underlying every word, every movement, an unspoken promise, a sense of belonging, even if it wasn't acknowledged as yet. Life had suddenly, miraculously, blossomed into something wonderful.

This was wartime. Time to live every day as if it were their last, as it might very well be. He had returned to her, but he had also returned to the danger the American airmen lived with every day. She would be a fool to waste this time fretting about morals and protocol and heritage. She would enjoy what they had, and if, when the time came, the obstacles proved too formidable for any permanent relationship between them, she would at least have these memories to enjoy. It was more than she'd expected a few short hours ago.

"I promise," she said softly. "And you promise me the same."

For his answer he lifted her hand and pressed his lips to her fingers. "You got it, your ladyship."

Earl left for the base immediately after their meal, with a promise that he'd be moving his things in that evening. As soon as his Jeep had disappeared, Elizabeth pulled on her coat and scarf and went out to the stables for her motorcycle.

Desmond was puttering around with a garden fork, even though the ground had to be as hard as a brick. Elizabeth suspected her gardener was just trying to look busy, since there wasn't that much to be done on the grounds in the midst of winter.

"You best be careful, m'm," he called out as she wheeled her motorcycle out of the stables. "Looks like another storm coming in off the ocean. It'll bring us another few inches of snow, I'm reckoning."

"Thank you, Desmond. I won't be long." Elizabeth eased her leg across the seat, wishing fervently she could wear trousers as so many of the young women were these days. So much warmer and more convenient.

Trousers, however, were still considered in the poorest taste for women, and a real lady would not be caught dead in them, as Rita Crumm was fond of saying.

Thinking of Rita Crumm usually put Elizabeth in a bad mood, but she was far too happy today to let even that harbinger of aggravation get her down. Even though the slate-gray clouds hid the sun, the world seemed brighter, cleaner, fresher, and full of hope and delicious anticipation.

She was smiling in the teeth of the bitter wind as she sailed down the coast road to the bay, where McNally had been renting one of the fishermen's cottages. The quaint little houses were actually owned by a building contractor in London and managed by Fred Shepperton's wife, Lydia.

Elizabeth sincerely hoped that the farmer's wife would not be attending to McNally's cottage that afternoon. If so, she would have to come up with a good excuse as to why she was there.

To her immense relief, the cottage appeared to be empty

when she rapped on the door. It was also locked, which presented a bit of a problem. Trotting around to the back of the house, Elizabeth tried all the windows. Fortunately she was shielded from the rest of the cottages by tall, thick laurel hedges.

The one-storey cottages had been renovated and updated by the contractor, and boasted indoor plumbing. Most of the older homes outside of the village relied on well water and outdoor facilities.

The lavatory window, as so often was the case in Elizabeth's experience, wasn't latched. It was a simple matter to lever it up high enough to accommodate her body. Reaching the sill to ease herself through the narrow space was another matter, however.

Her quick survey of the small garden was rewarded by the sight of a wooden window box that had been discarded and left on a compost heap in a shaded corner beneath a forlorn-looking oak tree. After shaking off a pile of acorns, Elizabeth carried the box to the window and placed it on the ground.

She had to stand it on end to give herself enough height, and it wobbled precariously as she climbed up and took hold of the sill. With a push of her feet she heaved her shoulders through the space. The window box fell over with a dull thud, but she was too intent on getting the rest of her body through the window and over the sink to worry about it then.

Entering a lavatory headfirst was not something she'd recommend, she reflected, as she struggled to unhook her skirt from the water taps. She could only pray that no one was able to see her legs waving wildly out of the window while she attempted to propel herself over the sink.

Once safely on the floor, she sat there for a moment or

two to catch her breath. This had seemed such a good idea at the time, but now that she was actually inside a locked cottage that didn't belong to her, she was beginning to realize the repercussions of being discovered in such an unethical position.

The best thing she could do was find the letters and get out of there as quickly as possible. Belatedly she realized that Douglas McNally might not have kept the offending letters, but now that she was there she should at least look for them.

A quick search of the front room revealed nothing, and the kitchen was equally unavailing. Elizabeth opened the door of the single bedroom and peeked inside. Obviously McNally hadn't been expecting visitors. While the front room and kitchen were reasonably clean, save for dirty dishes in the kitchen sink, his bedroom was another matter.

Clothes had been dropped onto the floor and left there. The bedclothes were flung back, as if he'd leaped out of bed in a hurry. The dressing table was piled high with books, papers, empty cigarettes packets, a half-filled bottle of Scotch, a camera, and several pairs of socks in need of darning. Feeling more uneasy by the minute at her unwarranted intrusion, Elizabeth sifted through the mess. There were several envelopes buried under the mound of books, and she drew them out.

Reading someone else's private post seemed even more meddlesome to her than sneaking into the cottage. Telling herself that the end would possibly justify the means, she slid the letter from the first envelope.

It was from a business associate of McNally's, and Elizabeth thrust it back in the envelope and replaced it under the books. The next one was a bill from the electric company, and a third was a letter asking McNally for a job at his factory. Elizabeth was intrigued to see it was written by Ray Muggins. According to his list of accomplishments, he seemed very qualified for the responsible job. No wonder McNally had hired him.

She thrust that letter back with the others and looked at the next one. This one bore an address in Scotland. Apparently McNally had deemed it important enough to bring with him. Her curiosity getting the better of her, Elizabeth took a peek at the letter inside.

It was written by Fred Shepperton, and Elizabeth's breath quickened as she read it. The farmer was angrily accusing McNally of misleading him. Apparently Shepperton had been warned by someone that the munitions factory would contaminate the land it was on and the pollution could spread to adjoining land. He was insisting that McNally cancel the deal.

Frowning, Elizabeth replaced the letter. Had McNally been able to reassure Shepperton that he'd been misinformed, or had the deal gone through despite Shepperton's demands? If the latter, the farmer had a strong motive to get rid of the factory and perhaps McNally with it.

Putting that letter aside for the moment, Elizabeth looked at the next letter. Her hand shook with excitement as she saw the envelope merely bore McNally's name and not his address.

Quickly she withdrew the sheet of paper inside and scanned the contents. The letter was brief and to the point. In capital letters it demanded, *CLOSE THE FACTORY AND TEAR IT DOWN OR YOU WILL DIE A HORRIBLE DEATH.*

Elizabeth shuddered. He had, indeed, died a horrible death. She found three more letters, all saying more or less the same thing, all written by a firm hand.

After finding no more among the pile, she picked up Shepperton's letter again. The handwriting was quite different, more clumsy and uneven than the neat printing of the unsigned letters. Even so, she placed it with the others in the pocket of her skirt and headed for the door.

She was halfway across the room when she heard a sound from somewhere in the cottage. Something fell with a tinkling of broken glass, followed by a harshly whispered curse.

There was no way, Elizabeth decided, that she could explain what she was doing in the dead man's bedroom. Not without arousing suspicions and alarm in the village. Her mind racing for a feasible excuse, she stared at the bedroom door and prayed whoever had entered the cottage had not come to make up the bed.

CHAPTER
❀ 8 ❀

Marge Gunther climbed the steps to the Manor House, wishing she'd worn her thick furry mittens instead of the thin gloves she'd knitted for herself. She'd walked up from the village, and her hands and feet were so cold they were numb.

She was beginning to think it was a big mistake to come up to the manor to get names on her list for the petition. When she'd first thought of it, she'd been excited about the brilliant idea. She, Marge Gunther, would be the only one to have the signature of the lady of the manor on her petition!

Rita had given her the cottages in the bay as her assignment, but who listened to fisherman's wives, anyway? Her petition would mean so much more if she could get Lady Elizabeth and her household staff to sign it. Just think how important that would be.

Now, however, after having climbed the hill in the bitter wind, Marge wished she'd gone down to the bay after all. She'd be back home by now, enjoying a nice hot cup of tea and one of the currant buns she'd bought from Bessie that morning.

Bessie's baking was fit for a king, and although no one was supposed to take the food out of the shop, the stuff being on rationing and all, Marge always managed to smuggle something out in her handbag so she could enjoy it at home later.

After all, everyone knew the constables bought stuff and took it back to the police station, even though they weren't supposed to; and if the bobbies could blinking well do it, then so could she.

Marge tugged on the bell rope, knowing she'd have a few minutes to wait before Martin took the long, torturous journey from his room, then up the stairs to the front door. Unless he was somewhere in the vicinity, which had never happened the few times she'd found an excuse to call on the manor.

Today was no exception. Shivering in the cold, Marge moved closer to the front door to escape the wicked bite of the wind. Her fingers were so numb she'd have trouble finding the pencil to give to her ladyship. Then again, Lady Elizabeth must have plenty of pens and pencils lying around her office.

Must be nice to have money, Marge thought, leaning her back against the door. Though living in a big house like this would have its problems. It must be drafty, for one thing. Take a lot of coal fires to heat this place up. And the housework! Just think how long it would take to clean a place this big.

Having decided she'd waited long enough, Marge

tugged on the bell rope again. She waited until the hollow echo of the bell had faded away, then gave it another tug for good measure.

Almost immediately she heard the sound of bolts being drawn back and latches lifted. Impatiently she waited, until the door opened a crack and Martin's wavering voice demanded, "May I ask who's calling?"

"It's me, Marge Gunther." Marge gave the door a hefty push. "I've come to see her ladyship."

A brief yelp of pain answered her and she winced. "Sorry. I didn't know you was standing that close to the door."

Martin's face appeared in the gap, one hand holding his nose. Tears stood in his eyes as he glared at her. "Her ladyship is not at home."

Disappointment made Marge's tone sharp. "Well, I suppose you'll have to do, then."

"I beg your pardon?" He sounded as if he had a bad cold, no doubt due to the hold he had on his nose.

"It's this petition." Marge held out the sheet of paper. "I would like you to sign it, please."

Martin regarded the paper with suspicion. "What is it?"

"It's a petition to close down the factory for good. It's an eyesore and . . . and . . ." she struggled to remember everything Rita had told them to say in order to get people to sign.

"A factory?" Martin looked confused.

"The one what burned down," Marge said impatiently. She was dying to go to the lav. The idea of asking this toffee-nosed bugger if she could use their lavatory was daunting, but when nature called this loudly she didn't have much choice.

While she was trying to phrase the request in her mind,

Martin said tartly, "If this factory, or whatever it is you're talking about, burned down, then why do you need a petition to close it? It hardly seems likely that anyone would have any use for it now."

"It didn't burn all the way down, did it." Marge felt her nose beginning to drip with the cold and she sniffed hard. "They're going to rebuild it. That's what the petition's for, to stop them building it up again."

"Why on earth would they want to build a factory in Sitting Marsh in the first place?"

Marge dabbed at her nose with the back of her gloved hand. "They're making guns and bullets and stuff there, that's why. Rita says as how it's a. . . ." she struggled for the word Rita had used. Rita was always using long words that nobody understood. "Magnet!" she said triumphantly. "That's the word. It's a magnet for the Germans."

Martin's sour look of disgust was beginning to annoy her. Mostly because she couldn't find her hankie and had to use her glove to wipe her nose. Not only that, the urge to piddle was reaching desperate proportions. She pressed her knees together. "I wonder if her ladyship would mind—"

"As I've mentioned already," Martin said haughtily, "her ladyship is not at home. Even if she were, I seriously doubt that she would sign a paper allowing Germans to come to Sitting Marsh to get their guns and bullets. Good day to you."

"The guns are not for the Germans you twerp—" Seeing the door closing on her, Marge stuck out her foot in the gap. "Here, I'm not finished."

"Oh, yes you are," Martin said. Unfortunately, he'd failed to see her foot in the door, or more likely, chose not to see it. Either way, the heavy door squashed Marge's toes, which were already numb with cold. The pain was excruciating, and her shriek was loud enough to be heard all the way down the hill to the village below.

The door swung open again and released her foot. A little too late as it turned out. The bruising pain had caused her to lose control, and, in great embarrassment, she watched the warm puddle form at her feet. It was going to be a really long, damp walk home.

The door to the bedroom opened, and Elizabeth held her breath. At the last minute she'd slithered under the bed, hoping that the tossed bedclothes would help to hide her from the visitor. One thing was obvious. McNally was no housekeeper. The dust had gathered in lumps and drifted past her nose with the draft. Any minute now she was going to let loose with a gigantic sneeze.

Lying on the hard floorboards, Elizabeth watched a pair of shoes walk across the rug in the direction of the dressing table. A woman, obviously. Probably young, judging from the thick, high sole of the platform shoes. Wearing nylons, too. The only place Elizabeth knew where one could obtain nylons was from the American base. She had to be a young woman.

Lydia Shepperton was over fifty years old and weighed at least twelve stone. Somehow Elizabeth doubted she'd be prancing around in high platform soles. She was dying to inch forward and get a look at the woman's face, but any movement was bound to give away her hiding place.

She was beginning to regret her impulsive move. It was one thing to explain what she was doing in Douglas McNally's cottage without permission. It was quite another to find a good reason why she should be lying under his bed.

The sound of scuffling and rustling told her that the

woman was sorting through the mess on the dressing table. *This must be the relative responsible for packing up McNally's things.* Though according to George, there would be three of them at least, and Elizabeth had the impression they would be older people.

While she was debating whether or not to chance a peek, something dropped to the floor with a thump. From where she lay, she could see it quite clearly. It was one of the books from the dressing table. As she watched, a hand came down to retrieve it—long, slim, and elegant.

Elizabeth shrank back as far as she could. Even so, a face dipped into view and then, just as quickly, disappeared. Luckily the visitor hadn't thought to look under the bed. It had been just a brief glimpse, but enough for Elizabeth to recognize the face.

It was Nellie Smith, the Housewives League's only unmarried member, and by the sounds of drawers being opened and closed, she was doing a thorough job of searching the bedroom.

It seemed an eternity while Elizabeth waited for the young woman to leave. Her prayers were answered when Nellie apparently deemed it unnecessary to search under the bed. Whatever it was she was looking for, she'd either found it or had given up, because she finally hurried out of the room and Elizabeth could crawl out from her self-imposed torture chamber.

Her shoulder ached from the pressure of the floorboards and she'd snagged her stocking on a broken spring, causing an ugly ladder to run up the length of her leg. Stretching her stiff limbs to restore the circulation, she reminded herself that now that Earl was back, perhaps she could once more enjoy the luxury of nylon stockings. Once a woman had worn the smooth, filmy garments, it was very difficult to feel elegant in the itchy lisle ones she was used to wearing.

A quick glance at the dressing table told her nothing about what might be missing. She would have given a great deal to know why Nellie was sorting through McNally's belongings. Could it be that Nellie was looking for the same thing she herself had come there to find?

Elizabeth brushed herself down and headed for the door. She found it very difficult to believe that the bright, vivacious young woman could turn out to be a cold-blooded killer. Then again, war did strange things to people. It turned young men into ruthless killers. Why not women, too?

The thought sickened her, and she hurried to the front door. She was about to open it when she realized she had no way of locking it behind her. She would have to go out the way she came in. Just to be sure, she tested it. It was securely locked. Apparently Nellie had entered the house the same awkward way she had.

Sighing heavily, Elizabeth returned to the lavatory. The window was now closed and she leaned forward to open it. The sink prevented her from seeing if the window box was still there. She would have to wait until she was on the window sill.

That was a little more trouble than she'd anticipated and she was feeling decidedly peevish by the time she'd scrambled through the gap in the window. The window box was there, but still lying on its side. Either Nellie hadn't needed to use it, or it had fallen again.

The drop to the uneven ground twisted Elizabeth's ankle, and she limped back to her motorcycle, wondering why on earth she took it upon herself to attempt such formidable tasks instead of allowing the constables to do their job.

The answer, she ruefully reminded herself, was that

George and Sid were either uninterested or unable to conduct a successful police investigation. If there was a murderer in the village, she had to do something about it. Perhaps if she showed the letters to George, it would be enough to goad him into investigating.

Since she had to pass the Tudor Arms on the way home, and since it was shortly before opening time at the pub, she decided to call on Alfie. The congenial barman was always gracious and accommodating, and could usually be relied upon to offer her a glass of her favorite cream sherry.

She found him behind the long, pitted counter as usual, priming the pumps for the evening rush of customers. He looked up to the sound of the tinkling bell as she entered, and nodded a greeting.

The odor of beer and stale cigarette smoke largely masked the musty smell of the ancient establishment. Having been built a few centuries ago, the thick oak beams stretching across the ceiling allowed scant headroom for anyone approaching six feet in height. Elizabeth smiled, remembering Earl's instinctive habit of ducking his head whenever he entered the pub through the low doorway.

She propped herself up on a bar stool and greeted the barman. "Good evening, Alfie. It's quite chilly out there tonight."

"Well, your ladyship, I reckon you need a drop of the old firewater then." He reached under the counter and came up holding a bottle of French cognac. "Only keep this for me special customers, I do."

Elizabeth's eyes widened. "Wherever did you manage to find that? I haven't seen cognac since the rationing started."

Alfie winked. "Ah, that'd be telling now, wouldn't it. Care for a drop?"

"Oh, I shouldn't really." Elizabeth wavered. "Well, perhaps a little spot of it. Thank you, Alfie."

"My pleasure, m'm. A little drop of what you fancy does you good, you know."

"I suppose so." Elizabeth took a cautious sip of the bronze liquid and choked as it seared her throat. "My goodness, this is potent," she said, when she could speak.

Alfie grinned happily at her. "Ah, that it is. Good stuff, that is."

"It is indeed." Elizabeth put the glass down. "Alfie, I was talking to George about that dreadful fire at the munitions factory."

Alfie's grin vanished. "Nasty business that were. Two people dead. Could have been a lot more if it had been in the daytime."

"Yes, I imagine you're right. I understand Fred Shepperton came down here to raise the alarm."

"That's right, m'm. Woke me up, he did, banging on the front door. Said he'd heard the explosion and came right down here on his bicycle."

"What time was that?"

Alfie gazed at the ceiling and stroked his chin. "Let's see. Must have been a little after midnight. I hadn't been in bed that long. I let Fred in and he used the telephone to ring the fire brigade, then went straight back to the factory to wait for them. Of course, we didn't know right then that there were two people inside."

"That must have come as a nasty shock to him."

"I reckon it did at that. Then again, what was McNally doing there at that time of night, that's what I want to know. I know Jessie's usually there until about one o'clock in the morning doing her cleaning, but why McNally was there that late's a mystery to me."

"You know, Alfie, you're the first person to mention that." Elizabeth picked up her glass. "That's something I'm curious about, too."

"Seem a bit late to be working. But then again, who knows. It just seems strange, don't it." Alfie started lining up the glass tankards on the counter.

"A lot of things seem strange." Elizabeth hesitated, then decided to keep to herself for the present the matter of the locked office door. "Violet was telling me that Jack Mitchum wasn't very happy about his wife working there."

"That's putting it mildly. They had a right barney about it down here. Jack and McNally that is. Millie wasn't here, or she'd have had her say as well."

Elizabeth sipped her brandy, relieved that it didn't burn the way her first sip had done. "I do hope it didn't come to blows."

"Well," Alfie looked around as if afraid to be overheard, even though no one else was in the pub. "Jack'd had a few pints of wallop by then, and sometimes he gets a little bombastic, if you know what I mean."

Elizabeth nodded. She knew exactly what he meant. She'd witnessed Jack Mitchum's temper more than once.

"Anyway, Jack said he didn't like Millie working at the factory. He said her place was in the butcher's shop with him. McNally said he reckoned Millie was old enough to make her own decisions and that she could earn good money working in the factory."

"And Jack took offense to that?"

"You bet he did. He accused McNally of having his eye on Millie. You know how Millie is. She likes a laugh with the blokes, all right. Well, McNally got upset about that and shouted right back at Jack. Said it wasn't his fault if Millie was tired of working for a selfish bully."

"Oh, dear."

"Well, then Jack said as how McNally was trying to destroy the village and should go back to Scotland where he belonged and take his factory with him." Alfie grinned sheepishly. "To be honest, he used some bad words in there, but I left them out so as not to shock you, m'm."

"I appreciate that, Alfie." Elizabeth took another delicate sip of the brandy. The drink was actually feeling quite pleasant now, sliding down and warming her stomach. "So what happened then?"

Alfie shrugged. "Nothing much. McNally muttered something and took his beer over to his table. Jack stayed right here at the counter for a while, then went off to play darts. I don't think they spoke to each other after that."

Elizabeth drained her glass. "Well, thank you, Alfie. I suppose I'd better be getting along. I'd rather not be here when your customers start arriving."

"I understand, m'm. Though people don't seem to take much notice anymore if ladies come into the pub. As long as it's the lounge bar, of course, and not the public bar."

Elizabeth shuddered. "I can assure you, I would not be caught dead in the public bar. As for being here in the lounge bar, I still feel uncomfortable coming in here unescorted."

Alfie reached up to the rack of glass tankards above his head and took two of them down. "Times are changing, your ladyship. Already some of our local girls are taking on the blokes at the dartboard. Your Sadie, for instance. Getting to be quite a dead-eye Dick, she is."

"Yes, well, Sadie is from the East End. They tend to be a lot more permissive in that part of London. What's left of it, that is, after the Blitz practically flattened it."

Alfie nodded, his face serious. "She were lucky to come

out of that alive. Killed no end of people, them Nazis. They should all be burned alive, that's what I say."

That was a little too much of a reminder of what had happened to poor Douglas McNally. In her haste to get off the stool, Elizabeth lost her footing and landed on her sore ankle, which immediately buckled under her. She managed to grab the counter and regain her balance, only to find Alfie gazing at her in concern.

"Are you all right, your ladyship? Not getting tipsy, are we?"

Embarrassed, Elizabeth wound her scarf around her head and, with as much dignity as she could muster, murmured, "Emphatically not. I twisted my ankle earlier today, that's all."

"Are you going to be all right to ride that motorcycle home?" Alfie glanced at the clock. "I have the beer lorry outside. I could run you up the hill if you like."

"Thank you, Alfie, but that won't be necessary. I can manage perfectly well." She bid him goodnight and headed for the door, doing her level best not to limp. Just as she reached the door, it opened and a group of GIs stood back to let her pass.

"Leaving already?" one of them asked, with a lurid wink at her.

Elizabeth merely smiled and hurried past them. There was only one American she was interested in, and she simply couldn't wait to see him again.

All the time she thought he wasn't coming back she'd managed to smother her feelings under a blanket of self-righteous assurances that his departure had been the best thing for everyone concerned.

But now things were different. Very different. It was all

she could do not to fling herself around in circles screeching to the heavens in joyful gratitude to the powers-that-be for bringing him back to her.

She might have done that very thing if it wasn't for the dull ache in her ankle and, of course, the sobering fact that if people saw the lady of the manor behaving with such a lack of decorum, they would assume she had quite lost her mind. Or worse, assume that she had imbibed more than her fair share of Alfie's firewater.

Having successfully kick-started the engine on her motorcycle, a maneuver Violet considered utterly crude and inelegant, Elizabeth zoomed out of the car park and up the coast road.

The daylight was fading fast as she sailed up the hill, and the wind whipped at the scarf she'd tucked across her nose and mouth. She barely noticed the cold, however. Her mind was busily replaying the afternoon's events. It had been an enlightening day. She had started out with no suspects, and now she had at least three.

Fred Shepperton had good reason to be rid of the factory. As did Jack Mitchum. But enough to kill in such a horrible way? If it hadn't been for the locked door, she might have thought either one of them capable of setting fire to the place. But it seemed very much as if someone had deliberately seen to it that McNally had died in that fire, unfortunately taking Jessie with him.

What about Nellie? Had she been searching for the threatening letters? If so, it seemed feasible to assume that either she had written them, or that she knew who had and was protecting him.

Cold-blooded murder. It was hard to believe that any one of the suspects was capable of such a heinous crime.

Elizabeth let out her breath into the warm fuzz of her scarf.
The fact remained that someone was responsible and had
to be punished for the deaths of two innocent people. No
matter the cost.

CHAPTER
❦ 9 ❦

Early the following morning, Elizabeth was halfway down the front steps when she saw a figure peddling a bicycle furiously down the driveway. To her surprise, she saw it was Nellie Smith, and for a wild moment she wondered if Nellie had spotted her in the cottage after all and was coming to confront her about it.

She waited until the young woman had dismounted from her bicycle and leaned it against the wall before going down the steps to greet her.

Nellie's face was flushed from her exertion, and strands of her blonde hair had escaped from her wooly scarf and were plastered to her forehead. She was out of breath, and her words came out in little gasps as she held out a fluttering sheet of paper. "I was wondering, your ladyship, if you'd sign this petition. I've got a pencil here for you somewhere."

Elizabeth took the paper while Nellie hunted feverishly through the pockets of her thick coat. Quickly she scanned the hand-printed lines and the heavily scrawled signature at the bottom. *Rita*. Of course. "I'm sorry," she said, handing the paper back to Nellie. "I'm afraid I can't sign this."

Nellie's face creased in dismay. "But I cycled all the way up the hill. It's important. We've got to close the factory down or the Germans will bomb the village. And it's ugly, and it spoils the countryside."

"Even if I agreed with you," Elizabeth said evenly, "I couldn't sign it. I'm bound by the councilors' decision and they voted for the factory by a wide majority."

Nellie's eyes narrowed. "There's only five members on the council, your ladyship."

"Well, yes," Elizabeth admitted. "Four to one, however, could be considered a wide majority."

"That factory has already caused the death of two people," Nellie said, obviously having been well-rehearsed by her stalwart leader. "How many more have to die before people come to their senses and get rid of it?"

Elizabeth studied the young woman's face. Was this all an act to cover up her own connection to the tragedy? Deciding it was time to take a risk or two, she said quietly, "Nellie, I happened to see you go into Mr. McNally's cottage yesterday."

The girl's face turned a bright red. Abandoning all effort of observing protocol she muttered, "So what if I did?"

"I was wondering why you felt it necessary to break into the cottage," Elizabeth said, conveniently neglecting to admit she had broken in there first. "After all, if there were something in there you needed, surely it would have been better to ask permission to retrieve it?"

"I didn't break in," Nellie said defiantly. "The window was open and I went through it."

"Entering someone's private abode without permission is the same as breaking in. I think P.C. Dalrymple would agree with me." *Really,* she thought wryly, *I am becoming quite a hypocrite.* Her only defense was that she was acting under the jurisdiction of her position and the need to apprehend a possible murderer. It didn't entirely soothe her conscience, but it helped.

Nellie gazed at her in alarm, all signs of her rebellion vanishing. "You don't have to tell the bobbies, m'm. I didn't take anything."

"Because you couldn't find what you were looking for? Such as some letters, perhaps?"

Nellie's eyes widened. For a long moment she seemed speechless, then she blurted out, "I don't know what you're taking about."

"I think you do," Elizabeth said gently.

Looking thoroughly shaken, Nellie sank onto the bottom step and buried her face in her gloved hands. "I didn't want anyone to know. That's why I went in there without asking. I just wanted to get them back, that's all. But they weren't there. I couldn't find them. I never touched anything else."

"I'm sure you didn't." Elizabeth seated herself on the step next to the girl. "I won't say any more about you breaking into the cottage if you'll just tell me who wrote the letters."

Nellie looked at her in surprise. "Well, I did, m'm. I thought you knew that."

Cold horror crept down Elizabeth's spine. She hadn't allowed herself to believe that this young person could be capable of such a vicious act, but to hear her admit she wrote the threatening letters in such a matter-of-fact way made it seem all the more horrendous.

Still unable to accept that Nellie was responsible for the deaths, Elizabeth asked warily, "You wrote the letters to Douglas McNally?"

Nellie nodded, her teeth worrying at her bottom lip. "I know it seems like we hadn't known each other long, but I met him when he first came down here to look for the land to build the factory. He didn't know many people here, and I felt sorry for him. So I went out with him."

Elizabeth stared at her in amazement. "I didn't know that."

Nellie shrugged. "Well, we kept it quiet, see, on account of him being so much older than me. He was sort of funny about that. Didn't want people to think he was robbing the cradle."

"I see." Elizabeth still had trouble picturing the vivacious young girl with the dour Scotsman. "So you knew Mr. McNally quite well."

"Very well." Nellie looked down at her gloved hands. "After he went back to Scotland, we wrote to each other. Really friendly letters, if you know what I mean."

Elizabeth nodded. "I think so."

"Well, anyway, I thought things were going smashing between us, and when Douglas said he was coming back to Sitting Marsh to build the factory, I got really, really excited." She sighed. "I even started thinking about getting married."

"But Mr. McNally didn't feel the same way," Elizabeth ventured.

"That's right. He said he'd had time to think about it while he was away and he decided he was too old for me. He said as how I'd do better with a young chap because we'd have more in common." She uttered a bitter laugh. "The only young blokes around here are either Yanks or in the army. I'm twenty-four years old. I'll be a bloody old maid before this war is over."

Suddenly feeling ancient, Elizabeth squirmed. "So that's why you wrote the letters Mr. McNally received recently."

"Well, I don't know about recent." Nellie scuffed the snow with the toe of her boot. "At first I was silly about it, and kept writing to him begging him to take me back. Then, when he wouldn't change his mind, I got so bloody mad at him." She glanced up at Elizabeth. "Pardon me, m'm."

Elizabeth was too upset to worry about the girl's curses. "I'm sure you didn't really mean what you said in the letters, though."

Nellie stared at her. "Of course I did."

Now Elizabeth was in a spot. She couldn't admit she knew what was in the letters without also admitting she was actually inside the cottage herself. Searching for the right words, she said hesitantly, "Nellie, people say a lot of things when they're angry. That doesn't mean they would carry out their threats. I'm sure whatever you wrote to Mr. McNally in anger—"

"Just a minute!" Nellie looked quite put out. "I never wrote any angry letters to Douglas. Once I realized he didn't want nothing more to do with me, I stopped writing to him. I wouldn't have given him the satisfaction of letting him know how much he hurt me."

Elizabeth swallowed hard. "So you didn't write and threaten to kill him?" Nellie looked so shocked, she added quickly, "Or something like that?"

"Of course not, m'm. What'd you take me for? No man is worth going to all that—" She broke off, her eyes widening. "What, are you saying someone wanted to kill Douglas?"

"Certainly not." Elizabeth pretended to be appalled. "I wouldn't suggest such a thing. Not at all." She was protesting too much, she warned herself. "No, I was merely thinking aloud, that's all. After all, people do silly things when they're heartbroken."

"You mean women do," Nellie said gloomily. "Nothing like that seems to bother men, do it? Anyway, I wasn't really heartbroken. I reckon it was my pride that got hurt, because after a while I didn't care that much anymore. Of course, I was upset when I heard Douglas had died in that fire. I started thinking about his family coming down to fetch all his things and I didn't want them finding all those dopey letters I'd sent him. I didn't want people in the village finding out I'd made such a fool of myself, begging him and everything."

"So you went looking for them in the cottage."

Nellie nodded. "I didn't find them though. He must have thrown them away. Just shows how little he cared about me."

"Perhaps he just wanted to spare you embarrassment," Elizabeth said, rising to her feet.

"Well, it don't matter anymore, do it?" Nellie looked up. "There's just one thing I don't understand."

"And what's that?"

"How did you know about the letters?"

She should have been prepared for the question, but she wasn't. Seconds ticked by while she sought the right answer. At last she said weakly, "Mr. McNally mentioned someone had been writing to him, but he didn't say who it was. When I saw you going into the cottage, I guessed he was talking about you and that you would want the letters back."

It wasn't exactly a lie, she assured herself, just a slight distortion of the truth. Nellie still looked confused, but apparently decided to accept the flimsy explanation. She got to her feet, rubbing her hands together. "Well, I've taken up enough of your time, your ladyship."

Elizabeth smiled. "Not at all. I regret that I can't sign the petition, after you came all this way."

"Oh, that's all right, your ladyship." Nellie sat astride her bicycle. "I'm glad I came. It helped to talk about it. I couldn't talk about it to anyone else. Can you imagine what those old biddies in the Housewives League would say if they knew? I'd never hear the last of it."

"Well, rest assured, I shan't mention this to anyone," Elizabeth promised her. "Nellie, don't give up hope of meeting the right man. Sometimes things happen in the most unexpected ways."

"I know." Nellie's smile was wistful. "But sometimes I get lonely, m'm. Since my mum died and my dad got married again I've been on my own. It would be nice to have someone to share things with and take me places."

"I'm sure you'll find someone," Elizabeth said warmly.

She watched the young woman pedal down the driveway on her bicycle, understanding now that Nellie was simply searching for love. Having found it so recently herself, Elizabeth could only wish her well.

Having eliminated one of her suspects, Elizabeth decided her next visit should be to the Shepperton's farm. Fred Shepperton's letter to McNally had made it clear that he was angry with the Scotsman. Although the handwriting in the farmer's letter didn't match that of the threatening letters, it would be a simple matter, even a prudent move, to disguise it.

Fred was repairing the farm's main gate when Elizabeth arrived, and he greeted her with warm surprise. He suggested they retreat to the warmth of the farmhouse, where he proceeded to make her a hot cup of cocoa.

"My wife has gone down to meet Douglas McNally's relatives," he explained, when he carried the tray into the parlor. "They arrived early this morning from Scotland, to collect his things."

Settled on a comfortable chair, Elizabeth removed her scarf and gloves. She wrapped her chilled fingers around the cup and said quietly, "Such a tragic loss. Mr. McNally was a good man."

"To some people, I reckon." The farmer seated himself opposite her on a worn settee. "Is that why you come to see me? To ask about the fire?"

"Well, yes, I was rather curious about it," she admitted.

"I thought so. Word's got around the village that you're asking questions. I thought it would only be a matter of time before you got to me."

Oh, dear, Elizabeth thought. So much for keeping her investigation a secret.

"After all," Shepperton added, "I was the one who rang the fire brigade."

He actually sounded put out that she had waited this long to talk to him, Elizabeth realized with surprise. She tried to sound casual about the whole thing. "I would just like to know exactly what happened. When two people die in such a dreadful way, it's useful to know if there's something we can do to avoid such a tragedy in the future."

Shepperton look baffled. As well he might. She was stringing words together to avoid alerting him to her true purpose.

"Well," he said, "I don't know as how I can help you that much. I heard the explosion, got out of bed, threw some clothes on, saw the factory was in flames, got on my bicycle, and toddled off down to the pub to ring the fire brigade." He reached for a pipe sitting next to him on the arm of the chair.

"First time I've had to use the emergency number. Did you know it rings right through to North Horsham? Doesn't go to our police station here at all."

"Yes, well, I suppose it wouldn't. After all, George and Sid go home at the end of the day. There's no one in the police station at night to answer the telephone."

Shepperton fingered a hunk of tobacco from a tinfoil packet and jammed it into the bowl of his pipe with his thumb. "The chap who answered the telephone told me he'd ring George at home. Don't make sense, do it? I'm right here in Sitting Marsh, I ring for the fire brigade, it goes all the way to North Horsham and then has to come all the way back here to wake up our own constable."

"Then again, the fire brigade is in North Horsham," Elizabeth pointed out.

The farmer struck a match, held it to the mound of tobacco, and sucked, making a smacking noise with his lips. After a moment, a coil of smoke rose from the pipe, and the aroma of tobacco filled the room. "Aye," he said, nodding his head, "I reckon that do make sense, after all."

Glad they had established that, Elizabeth cleared her throat. "Mr. Shepperton, I understand you were unhappy about leasing your land to Mr. McNally."

Shepperton went on sucking at his pipe, but his eyes flicked up to give her a shrewd look when he answered, "'T'ain't no secret. When I said McNally could lease the land for his munitions factory, he forgot to mention that my land could be contaminated. Not just where the factory is, though that would have been bad enough. Could mean all the surrounding land as well. That'd ruin me. No doubt about that."

"Did you talk to Mr. McNally about it?"

Shepperton puffed out a cloud of smoke and leaned back

in his chair. "That I did. He said it was all nonsense. Showed me a bunch of papers claiming that the factory was safe and wouldn't do any damage to the land."

"That didn't convince you?"

"No, it didn't. These big business chaps will lie through their teeth to get what they want. I told him I wanted my land back and I wanted him gone. Him and his factory."

"What did he say to that?"

"He said it was too late to back out and I was stuck with him until the end of the war."

"I see."

"I know what you're thinking, your ladyship, and you'd be wrong. I didn't set that fire. I might have been a bit of a hothead in my youth, but I know right from wrong. And two wrongs don't make a right. I was going to fight this the legal way, with a solicitor and everything, but the fire saved me the trouble."

Elizabeth was inclined to believe him. Nevertheless, she withdrew one of the letters from her handbag and handed it to the farmer. "Do you, by any chance, recognize this handwriting?"

His shock was genuine. The pipe slipped from his mouth and he grabbed it, the hand holding the letter trembling. "Where did you get this?" he demanded.

"From Mr. McNally," Elizabeth said, sliding by the truth again. "He was concerned about the threats. He told me about them shortly before he died."

"Well, I'll admit there's a few of us in the village who think someone might have deliberately set fire to the factory. It's no secret a lot of people didn't want it there, and that would be a right good way to get rid of it. But murder? Now, that's something else. I just can't believe someone would deliberately kill McNally." Shepperton gave a decisive shake of his head. "If someone did set that fire, he most likely thought the building was empty."

"Except for Jessie Bandini and Captain Carbunkle. Both of whom were usually there late."

"Well, Jessie usually leaves around midnight or so. As for Wally, he wasn't supposed to be asleep in the building. He was supposed to be guarding it. If he'd done his job properly, McNally and Jessie wouldn't have died."

"Perhaps." Elizabeth held out her hand for the letter. "I agree, there may not be a connection between these letters and Mr. McNally's death. On the other hand, it's too much of a coincidence not to question it."

"What I don't understand," Shepperton stuffed the pipe back in his mouth and began talking with it through clenched teeth, "is why McNally and Jessie didn't get out of there. They must have heard the explosion."

Elizabeth considered telling him about the locked door, then decided to keep that bit of information to herself. If word got around the village, as it certainly would, the guilty person would know she was on the track, making things more difficult for her. Already she was treading on dangerous ground, now that everyone knew she was investigating the fire.

Still, she told herself as she made her way back to the manor, it wouldn't be the first time she'd courted danger. It most likely wouldn't be the last, either. Now that Earl was back in her life, her task didn't seem nearly as formidable as it had a day or two ago.

Feeling hungry, she was anticipating her midday meal when she arrived home. The fragrance of something savory wafting through the hallway intensified her appetite, and even Martin seemed in a hurry to get down to the kitchen.

He'd managed to get the front door open with more alacrity than usual. Having greeted Elizabeth, he speeded up his shuffling gait to such an extent that he had trouble slowing down when he reached the steps to the kitchen.

Elizabeth had quite a bad moment when she thought he might fall down them, but he showed remarkable presence of mind by bumping into the wall instead, thus halting his progress. He stood for a moment, shook his head, then proceeded at a more comfortable pace down the stairs.

Satisfied that her butler was still in one piece, Elizabeth headed for the stairs to the office. There was one person she needed to talk to before she could relax and enjoy her meal.

Just as she reached the stairs, Polly appeared at the top. She was clinging to the arm of a young man, and hastily let him go when she saw Elizabeth standing at the bottom. "Oh, there you are, m'm," she called out. "I wondered where you was."

No doubt hoping I wouldn't return this soon, Elizabeth thought, watching the two of them descend toward her.

"I was just showing Ray around the manor," Polly said, her cheeks flushed. "I hope that's all right, m'm?"

"Of course it is." She smiled at the young man. "How do you do."

Ray Muggins was a husky young man with greased black hair. He was a little too round-shouldered for someone his age, and had dark eyes that danced with mischief. His features were pleasant enough, but Elizabeth could see no resemblance to Humphrey Bogart as Polly had declared. Perhaps it took a little romance to see that.

He smiled and gave her a courteous little bow that she found quite charming. "Ray Muggins. It's a very great pleasure to meet you, your ladyship." He gazed around the hallway with awe on his face. "I appreciate you allowing me to view your magnificent home." His London accent wasn't at all cultured, but he managed to sound polished in spite of it.

"I hope Polly has explained some of our history," Elizabeth said, pleased to see the sparkle in her assistant's eyes. For far too long Polly had been grieving over Sam Cutter's departure. It was good to see the young girl brighten up at last.

"Oh, yes, your ladyship. She certainly has." Ray glanced over his shoulder up the stairs. "She told me all about the people in the portraits hanging in the great hall."

"Only the good things," Polly added hastily.

"I'm glad to hear it," Elizabeth murmured, reflecting on the misdeeds of some of her less noble ancestors. She turned back to Ray. "I'm so sorry about the tragic loss of Douglas McNally. I understand you were quite fond of him."

The stark look in Ray Muggins's eyes disturbed her. He dropped his gaze and his voice was unsteady when he answered. "It's terrible. I still can't believe he's gone."

She felt a rush of sympathy. "It must have been a shock to hear that the factory was on fire."

"It was." He took a breath, as if trying to ease his tension. "I was asleep when I heard the commotion downstairs. Fred Shepperton was pretty excited, and that booming voice of his echoed all the way up the stairs."

For a moment Elizabeth was confused, then understanding dawned. "Oh, you're staying at the Tudor Arms?"

Ray glanced at Polly. "That's right. Got the best room in the house. The only one where you can get a look at the sea from the window. I was going to find a place to rent, but now that the factory is closed I'll probably go back to London. Not much work down here, is there."

Polly looked stricken, and Elizabeth said quickly, "Oh, but there are plans to rebuild the factory. I'm sure it won't take long to repair the damage done by the fire. Perhaps you could find something in North Horsham until it's opened again."

"Yeah," Polly said eagerly. "I bet there's lots of jobs in North Horsham."

"We'll have to see." His eyes avoided Elizabeth's.

"Polly tells me you were at the factory when the fire brigade arrived," Elizabeth said, guiding the conversation back to where she wanted it.

Ray was obviously reluctant to talk about it. "I heard Shepperton ringing the fire brigade," he said, his voice low and muffled. "So I got up and got dressed and took my bike up there." He shook his head, as if trying to erase the memory. "There were flames coming out the roof, then part of it caved in. I never saw nothing like it. Sparks shooting up in the sky like rockets. By the time the brigade got there, the fire had a pretty good hold."

"You were there when they found Mr. McNally and Jessie in the office, then."

There was a long pause before he answered this time. "I couldn't believe it. He should never have been working there that time of night."

"Do you have any idea why he was working so late that night?" Elizabeth asked gently. She hated to pursue the questions when the young man was obviously devastated by the tragedy, but it was possible he had some vital answers to things that were puzzling her.

Ray lifted his shoulders in a shrug. His face was drawn with pain, and he gazed up at the ceiling as if searching for an answer. "I don't have the foggiest idea. He'd hang around sometimes after everyone had gone, just to finish up something, but I don't know how late he stayed. He could have been there to check up on Wally. Make sure he wasn't asleep on the job. Wally wasn't that reliable, you know. Douglas talked about catching him off guard one night. Maybe that was it."

"Polly told me you sometimes worked overtime."

"Just one night, that's all. I like to get out once my work day is done. The people I was training all went home, so there was nothing much for me to do anyway. The only time I stayed over was to finish up our first order. It was running late because people were still learning the assembly lines, so I stayed to help finish it, that's all. That was a week before the fire."

"Did Mr. McNally usually lock his office when he went home at night?"

Ray looked uneasy. "I can't say for sure, but I should think he would. After all, all the plans for the weapons were in a safe in his office. I reckon he'd want to keep it locked up."

"But he didn't keep it locked in the daytime?"

"I don't think so." The young man's gaze had sharpened with suspicion. "Excuse me, your ladyship, but why all the questions? Is there something going on I should know about?"

"Not really." Elizabeth gave him a reassuring smile. "I just like to know all the details, that's all."

"Because if there is," Ray went on, "if you think someone was up to no good that night, I'd really like to help find out what went on."

Surprised by the offer, Elizabeth murmured, "Thank you, Ray. I'll keep that in mind."

"Please do, m'm. After all, poking around in a place like that could be dangerous. We wouldn't want anything bad to happen to you, too, would we, Polly?"

Polly looked shocked. "Oh, no, m'm. We certainly wouldn't. Please be careful."

"I'm always careful," Elizabeth assured her assistant.

"Well, I must be off." Ray nodded at Elizabeth. "Thank you again, your ladyship. You have a lovely home."

"My pleasure." Elizabeth watched him leave with Polly. She'd misjudged the young man. He seemed intelligent and thoughtful. Polly could do a lot worse.

For now, however, she had someone else on her mind. Someone who she hoped could shed some light on this puzzle and give her some answers. Right now she was walking down a blind alley, and something told her if she didn't find the answers soon, there could be a few nasty surprises waiting for her.

CHAPTER

❈10❈

Dr. Robert Sheridan was most accommodating when he finally came to the telephone. After apologizing for keeping Elizabeth waiting, he did not sound reluctant to answer her questions.

"Both Douglas McNally and Jessie Bandini died from smoke inhalation," he told her.

That brought her a measure of relief. At least they hadn't had to face the horror of the flames. "The key to the cottage is missing. Did you happen to find any keys on Mr. McNally?" she asked. With any luck, the doctor wouldn't realize that the cottage was not on her estate.

"Keys?" There was a slight pause, then he added, "No, I didn't find any. But then lots of people don't carry their house key with them. In case they lose it, I suppose. Perhaps he left it under the mat?"

Elizabeth let out her breath. "Perhaps," she said. "I'll look for it." She thanked him and replaced the receiver in its cradle. No key. The question was, if the office door was locked, where was the key now?

If McNally had locked the door himself, which Elizabeth seriously doubted, and the key wasn't found on him, then it should still be in the office. There was only one way to settle that question. She would have to go to the factory and look for it herself.

Having decided that, she made her way down to the kitchen. Martin was already seated at the table, and he dragged himself to his feet as Elizabeth entered. Polly and Sadie were deep in discussion, while Violet stood at the stove busily stirring the source of the tantalizing fragrance Elizabeth had smelled earlier, which turned out to be a lamb stew.

The meal was a lively affair, with Sadie recounting her night out with Joe. "He took me out to a social at the base," she told Elizabeth. "It was fun but I felt so sorry for poor Joe. The lads were all teasing him something dreadful, they were."

"What for?" Polly asked.

"Because he's so backward in coming forward." Sadie uttered her raucous laugh. "If I didn't grab him and plonk one on his lips, he'd never kiss me goodnight."

Seated next to her, Violet glared at Sadie, while Martin choked on his stew. Polly giggled, earning her own glare from Violet.

Sadie shot Elizabeth a sheepish glance. "Didn't mean no disrespect, m'm."

"That's quite all right, Sadie." Elizabeth laid down her

spoon on her empty plate. "I hope you both managed to enjoy the evening."

Sadie nodded, her eyes glowing. "We had a smashing time. Joe's a really good dancer, though he don't say much. I have to drag everything out of him. He's frightened of saying the wrong thing. I don't think he's had a real girlfriend before. I'm his first one."

"Heaven help the poor blighter," Martin muttered.

Sadie ignored him. "Know what he told me, m'm? He said that Major Monroe is back and moving into the manor."

Elizabeth did her best to sound unaffected. "Yes, that's right. I believe the major moved in last night."

"Bet you're head over heels about that, m'm." Sadie grinned happily.

"That's none of your business, my girl," Violet snapped, saving Elizabeth the embarrassment of answering.

Sadie shrugged. "I was just thinking that now Polly's got a new boyfriend and the major's back and I've got Joe; everyone's got someone now." She smiled sweetly at Violet. "Except you, Violet. When are you going to get hooked up with a nice man?"

Violet's thin face turned the color of a beetroot. "What impudence! If you can't keep a decent tongue in your head, Sadie Buttons, you will be taking your meals in your own room in the future."

"I was just trying to—"

"Never mind what you were trying," Violet interrupted her. "None of this is your business and I'll thank you to keep a still tongue."

Martin sniffed. "You might as well ask the earth to stop revolving around the sun."

Violet gave him one of her lethal looks. "I don't remember asking for your opinion, neither."

Thankfully, just as Elizabeth was trying to think of a way to change the subject, Polly came to the rescue. "Me and Sadie came up with a terrific idea," she said. "We're going to organize letters for the soldiers overseas. I wrote and asked Marlene to give me the names of soldiers who don't have anyone to write to them, and we're going to ask everyone in the village to write a letter to every one of them so they won't feel so lonely anymore."

"Oh, what a lovely idea!" Elizabeth beamed at the two girls. "I'm quite sure the soldiers will appreciate that very much."

Even Violet seemed impressed by the idea, though she refrained from making a comment. She merely rose to gather up the empty dishes. Her silence on the subject indicated her approval, however.

"I asked Ray if he'd help us make posters that we could put up around the village," Polly went on, obviously caught up in this new venture. "We was wondering, m'm, if you had some paper we could use."

"Of course." Elizabeth handed her empty plate to Violet. "I have half a ream of full-sized sheets. They're on the shelf by the window. Just help yourself to what you need."

Polly nodded, her cheeks warm with excitement. "I know where they are. Thank you, m'm. Ray is looking forward to making the posters."

"Hope you'll have one ready by tonight," Sadie said. "We're supposed to go down the Arms to put one up on the wall, remember?"

"Ray said he'd make one up for us this afternoon." She looked at Elizabeth. "Would it be all right if I take the paper down to him? I'll be really fast on me bicycle."

"I'll drop it off for you," Elizabeth told her. "I'll be going right past there this afternoon."

"Oh, thank you, m'm." Polly turned to Sadie and grinned. "Looks like you and me will be putting up our first poster tonight."

"Your young man seems very nice," Elizabeth said, as she rose from the table.

Polly shrugged. "He's all right. He's nice enough, I s'pose."

"Give it time," Sadie told her. "From what you say he seems like a good bloke. You'll soon warm up to him and then you'll forget all about Sam."

"I'm never going to forget Sam," Polly said. "But Ray makes me laugh and he doesn't mind spending a bob or two. I suppose that's good enough for now."

Martin grunted, and everyone looked at him. He'd been struggling to his feet ever since Elizabeth had got up from the table, and only now was he upright, his gnarled hands resting on the table.

"Did you say something, luv?" Sadie inquired.

Martin scowled at her. "Even if I had been granted the chance to get a word in edgewise, I would not have lowered myself to address you, young lady. I have never heard such unmitigated piffle in my entire life. All this talk about consorting with men makes me quite ill."

" 'Ere," Sadie hotly protested. "What'd you mean, consorting? I hope you're not suggesting that I've been up to any monkey business, because I haven't. Not that it's any of your business if I had."

"It's all right, Sadie," Elizabeth said soothingly. "Consorting simply means socializing, that's all."

"Oh, well that's all right, then." Sadie eyed Martin with

suspicion. "I just don't want anyone getting any nasty ideas, that's all."

"Then perhaps you should reconsider your conversation at the dinner table," Martin said huffily.

"I think you girls should consider getting back to work." Violet looked pointedly at the clock. "The afternoon will be over before you get anything done."

Both girls promptly departed, leaving Elizabeth alone with Violet and her butler, who showed every sign of dozing off before he made it back to his room.

"Why don't you take your nap, Martin," Elizabeth suggested gently.

The old man nodded. "Thank you, madam. I do believe I shall. Please wake me in the event of an invasion. Or if we should have another bombing raid on the village."

"We haven't had any bombing raids on the village yet," Violet said sharply. "And if we did, the bombs would wake you up soon enough."

Martin peered at her over his glasses. "If we should become overrun by the Germans, Violet, I trust you will stand guard at the gates. One look at you and no doubt they will lay down their arms, turn tail, and run. If they have any sense at all, that is."

Violet rolled her eyes but wisely kept quiet as Martin shuffled from the room. Once the door had closed behind him, however, she muttered, "Silly old goat. He makes no sense at all."

Elizabeth smiled. "He thinks he does. And that's what counts." She headed for the door. "I shall be back before dark, as usual."

"Lizzie?"

Something in Violet's voice alerted Elizabeth, and she warily turned to face her housekeeper.

Violet actually seemed apprehensive as she stood wringing her hands, a frown wrinkling her brow. "I know this is none of my business," she said, "and you can tell me so when I'm done. But I've got to say this."

Anticipating what was coming, Elizabeth said quietly, "If this is about Major Monroe, Violet, I should warn you it's a sensitive subject."

Violet appeared to wrestle with indecision, then blurted out, "I just don't want you to go hoping for things that can't be, that's all. After what happened with you and Harry, I don't want to see you hurt like that again."

Violet meant well, Elizabeth reminded herself. The housekeeper had taken it upon herself to protect her employer after the death of Elizabeth's parents. At times that had been comforting, and at others, a little annoying, as it was now. Even so, she supposed she owed some kind of explanation to Violet. And now was as good a time as any.

"I'm not saying, at this point, that anything has changed between myself and Major Monroe," she said slowly. "But since you will find out eventually, you might as well know that he is getting divorced. It should be official in a few months."

Violet's mouth dropped open. "Does that mean," she said, after a long pause, "that you and the major . . . ?" She let her voice trail off, apparently unable to put the unthinkable into words.

"I don't quite know what it means right now," Elizabeth said truthfully. "Obviously the fact that Earl will no longer be married won't be the only consideration. I'm not going to pretend that I have no feelings for him. That would be pointless, anyway, since you know better."

Violet nodded, but the fear was naked on her face. "You

know I only want what's best for you, Lizzie. I just hope you know what that is."

"So do I." Elizabeth turned back to the door. "All I can say now is that no matter what happens, I shan't abandon you and Martin. I give you my promise. There are many hurdles to cross in the future. Right now I'm just taking things one day at a time. That's all any of us can do, really. There's no telling what the future might hold for us."

"Just be happy, Lizzie. That's all I ask."

Elizabeth gave in to the impulse and quickly crossed the room. Putting her arms around the frail figure of her housekeeper, she gave her a hug. "Happiness is such an elusive luxury, Violet," she said softly. "Let's just hope we get this war over with as quickly as possible, and that we all survive. I'll be happy enough with that."

"Amen." Violet sniffed, dabbing at her eyes with the back of her hand. "Now get off with you, or you'll never be home before the blackout."

Elizabeth's first stop was the Tudor Arms, and Alfie looked most surprised to see her walk in. "I was about to close up, your ladyship," he told her. "I'm sorry, but it's past two o'clock."

"Oh, I know it's past closing time," Elizabeth assured him. "I just came to deliver this paper to Ray Muggins. He's making posters for Sadie and Polly, I believe."

"Oh, you just missed him." Alfie held out his hand. "I'll take them, if you like. I'll give them to him when he comes in."

Elizabeth handed over the roll of paper. "Thank you, Alfie." She hesitated, aware that this was none of her business, but she couldn't ignore the opportunity to find out more about the young man Polly was dating. Although Polly lived with her mother, she spent more time at the Manor House than at home these days, and Elizabeth had always felt a strong sense of responsibility for the girl's welfare.

"Ray seems to be a nice young man," she said casually, as she fastened her wooly scarf a little more securely around her neck. "Polly gets along very well with him."

"He's all right, I suppose, m'm. Can't say as though I know much about him. Keeps himself to himself, if you know what I mean."

"It must be difficult for him to live in such a small village after being in London. Such a drastic change for him."

"Aye, that it is." Alfie started wiping down the counter with a wet cloth. "He seems to like it all right. He was really cut up about Douglas McNally's death, I do know that. His face were white as a ghost when he got back from the fire. Never seen a young bloke like him that upset. I thought he was going to cry when he told me about the firemen finding the body. I didn't realize he were that fond of his boss."

"From what Polly says, I think they were on very good terms. Apparently Ray recently lost his father and he regarded Mr. McNally as a substitute father. He certainly does seem to be a sensitive young man."

Alfie shrugged. "Like I said, m'm. I don't really know him. Deep. That's what I'd say. You never really know what he's thinking."

For some reason, that disturbed her, and she left the pub feeling that she'd like to know a lot more about Ray Muggins before she felt comfortable about Polly spending time with him.

Before she ventured out to the ruined factory, she needed to have word with Jack Mitchum. She had known the burly butcher for a good many years, and she couldn't imagine him committing cold-blooded murder, but he certainly had a motive.

She found him trussing chickens in the back of the shop when she entered. Fortunately there was only one customer in the shop at the time, and she was on her way out.

Recognizing one of Rita Crumm's league members, Elizabeth reluctantly exchanged greetings. Any time the lady of the manor took it upon herself to visit one of the local shops, it aroused speculation, whether deserved or not. This was one time when Elizabeth would have preferred to keep her visit quiet.

Millie Mitchum was behind the counter, and she greeted her visitor with obvious surprise. "Fancy seeing you here, your ladyship," she gushed. "This is an unexpected pleasure."

Elizabeth had planned on speaking to the butcher alone, but because Millie was indirectly involved, she decided she might as well talk to them both. Since she could be interrupted by another customer at any time, she came directly to the point.

"Shortly before his death, Douglas McNally received some rather nasty letters," she said, drawing one from her handbag. She handed it to Jack Mitchum, who hastily wiped his hands on his apron before taking it. "I was wondering if you recognized this."

"We heard about the letters, m'm," Millie said, sounding worried. "Nasty business, that."

The village grapevine had been working overtime, Elizabeth thought ruefully.

"What you're really asking," Jack Mitchum said, as he scanned the letter, "is if I wrote them."

Millie gasped, while Elizabeth gave him a direct look.

"I heard about the argument you had with Mr. McNally in the pub."

Mitchum nodded and handed the letter back to her. "Yes, I thought so."

"He didn't mean nothing by it," Millie said hastily. "It was all a misunderstanding, wasn't it, Jack."

"That's right." Mitchum folded his brawny arms across his chest. "We'd both had a few pints that night. I was fed up because Millie wanted to work in the factory instead of helping me in the shop. I need her here, and I told McNally so. He said that being my wife didn't make Millie my slave and she could do what she liked. I got ticked off about that. I said as how it was none of his business, and no more it weren't."

"I could see Jack's side of it," Millie put in. "He couldn't find anyone to help him in the shop. But I liked working in the factory, and I made good money. Or I would have if someone hadn't burned it down."

Apparently the villagers, at least, no longer thought the fire was an accident, Elizabeth noted. "But you didn't write the letters threatening Mr. McNally?"

Mitchum laughed. "If I'd wanted to have it out with him, I wouldn't have wasted my time with letters. I'd have been up there with a meat chopper."

"Alfie tells me you accused Mr. McNally of taking a personal interest in your wife." Elizabeth watched Millie's face, but the woman merely seemed disgusted.

"I might have done." Mitchum unfolded his arms and grabbed a chicken by the bony neck. "People say things when they're angry. Don't mean they mean anything by it. I'm not saying I liked him, but I didn't wish him any harm." He laid the chicken on the wooden block, picked up a chopper, and with a swift slash of the blade, neatly separated the bird from its head.

Elizabeth winced and swallowed hard.

"He didn't write those letters, your ladyship," Millie said earnestly. "I'd swear on my mother's grave to that."

"I didn't set no fires, neither," Mitchum said. "In fact, the last time I saw McNally was right here in this shop. We shook hands before he left."

"That's right," Millie chimed in. "I saw them do that. So did the customers who were in here. They'll tell you."

"That won't be necessary," Elizabeth said, tucking the letter back in her handbag. "In any case, there's nothing to suggest as yet that the fire was deliberately set. It's all conjecture, and I really think we should all remember that."

Both Millie and her husband gazed at her without answering, obviously keeping their own counsel on that score. She wasn't sure if she was convinced or not by their air of innocence, but it was quite apparent she wasn't going to learn any more from the Mitchums. She thanked them and left the shop feeling more confused than ever.

Maybe I am overreacting to all this, she thought, as she mounted her motorcycle once more. *Perhaps Douglas McNally did have a good reason to lock the office door that night. Maybe the fire was simply an unfortunate accident as Dave Meadows proclaimed.* She could accept that, perhaps, if it wasn't for the coincidence of the threatening letters, as well as the niggling feeling in the back of her mind that something didn't fit.

She'd had that feeling before. Many times. Each time she'd been proven right, and her suspicions had been realized. As long as she had that annoying little buzz in her mind, she could not ignore it. Her instincts were strong, and she had no choice but to follow them until she was satisfied.

Dusk was rapidly approaching as she rode her motorcycle down the High Street. It would be dark before she reached the factory, she realized. Apart from the hazards of riding a motorcycle without lights along a country road, she had to assume that there was no power in the building, which would make a search impractical. She would have to wait until the next day.

To her immense joy, Earl was waiting for her in the library when she returned to the manor.

"I've caught up on all the reports," he told her, "and we're grounded for the time being by the weather. So I'm at your disposal. For tonight, anyway."

"Then you must have dinner with me. I'll see if Violet has anything palatable in the pantry."

She started for the kitchen, but he caught her hand. "I've already talked to Violet. I gave her some steaks and a bottle of brandy. She was very happy to see me."

Elizabeth laughed. "You do have a way with you, Major. Though bribing the servants is rather unethical, don't you think?"

He grinned back at her. "Depends what results I get. As long as everyone's happy, a little bribery can sure go a long way."

She shook her head in mock disgust. "You'll be corrupting my household before too long."

He tucked her hand under his arm. "You're the only one I want to corrupt. Let's go down to the conservatory, so I can get started."

"Shame on you, Major. You would jeopardize the reputation of the lady of the manor?"

"Only if she's willing." His wink was pure lechery.

"You promised to keep your distance," she reminded him demurely, as they made their way to the conservatory.

Earl sighed. "So I did. That was pretty stupid of me."

"But ethical."

"Ah, there's that word again. How I'm beginning to hate that word."

Knowing he was teasing, she smiled up at him. Happiness might be elusive, she thought, but right this minute she was happier than anyone had a right to be. If only this feeling could last for the rest of her life, she'd never ask for anything more.

CHAPTER

❧11❧

"I thought you said that Ray would be waiting for you," Sadie said, raising her voice above the din in the pub.

"He'll be down in a minute." Polly peered at the clock across the room. "We're early. I said half past seven and it's only a quarter past."

"Well, I hope he hurries up. I'm dying to meet him." Sadie worked her way through a group of GIs at the bar, ignoring their ribald comments. Polly squeezed through behind her and refused to look at any of the airmen. After what happened with Sam she'd made up her mind she was never going to look at another Yank.

Sadie had reached the bar and was talking to Alfie, who was busily filling tankards with foaming ale from the pumps. "So is it all right if we pin up the poster?" she said, her voice raised to be heard.

An American standing next to her leered at her. "You got a pinup poster? Betty Grable, I bet."

Sadie gave him a dirty look. "No, it's not a pinup, so take that smarmy look off your face."

The Yank laughed, and wound his arm around her waist. "Come on, honey. Don't be like that. How about a cuddle with a lonely GI far from home?"

Sadie wriggled free and shoved the American's chest with both hands. "Sod off and leave me alone. I've already got a boyfriend, and he's a lot better-looking than you."

The Yank laughed again, then he turned to Polly. "All right, then, how about you, sweetheart? Ready for a good ol' roll in the hay?"

Polly opened her mouth to deliver a scathing reply, but from out of nowhere Ray's voice came harshly: "Leave her alone."

Relieved, she started toward him, but the Yank had other ideas. He grabbed hold of her arm and dragged her close to him. "Who's going to make me?"

"Oh, blimey, here it comes," Sadie muttered.

Alfie left the pumps and moved to the middle of the counter. "All right, lads," he shouted. "Let's all calm down now, nice and quiet."

Polly struggled to get free, then everything happened at once. Ray's fist shot out and caught the Yank squarely on the nose. He let out a howl and let go of Polly's arm. Ray dragged her out of the crowd with Sadie right behind, but before he got too far, the GIs were on him.

A group of British soldiers had just entered the pub, and they flung themselves joyfully into the fray. Polly shoved her way out of the flying fists and looked around for Sadie. She was over by the door, pinning up a poster on the wall next to it.

Polly reached her as she pushed in the last pin, and together they went out the door.

"Where'd you get the poster?" she demanded.

"Ray had it. I snatched it from him when he punched that bugger in the nose."

Polly looked back at the door. "I should go back and see if he's all right."

"He'll be all right." Sadie buttoned up her coat. "He looks as if he can take care of himself."

"Sam did that for me once," Polly said. "He got in a fight over me in the pub. I left him fighting in there and I never did feel right about it. I'm going back in there."

Sadie sighed. "All right, I'll come, too."

"You don't have to." Polly winced as something inside the pub fell with a crash.

Sadie tucked her hand in Polly's arm. "We're mates, aren't we? We stick together."

Mates. Polly liked that. She grinned up at her friend. "All right. Let's go sort out them bloody Yanks."

"They will probably be bloody and all by the time this is over." Sadie pushed open the door, and the noise of the battle blasted their ears. "We'll need a suit of armor to get in there!"

Polly didn't answer. She was watching in amazement as her new boyfriend flattened a GI with a solid punch in the stomach. If she hadn't seen it with her own two eyes, she would never have imagined the quiet-spoken, polite young man could be so good with his fists. She was finding out all sorts of surprising things about Ray Muggins.

. . .

"What's new in the village?" Earl asked, after he'd settled Elizabeth on a chair at the long dining room table. "How's the investigation going?"

"It's not going anywhere." Elizabeth shivered. "It's awfully cold in here." She glanced across the dining room at the glowing coals in the fireplace. "If I'd known you were going to join me for dinner tonight, I'd have asked Desmond to light the fire this afternoon. It takes so long for the room to heat up, by the time it's comfortable it's time to go to bed."

Earl dragged a chair closer to her and sat down. "I can think of ways to keep us warm."

She flicked him a glance from beneath her lashes. "Behave yourself. Martin will be in with the dishes any minute. If he heard you talking like that he'd have a heart attack."

Earl sighed. "You're spoiling all my fun."

"You promised."

"I know. I didn't think it would be this tough."

She smiled. "We've waited this long. We can wait a few more months."

The expression in his eyes worried her. "I hate to waste this time," he said quietly. "Things are so unpredictable in wartime."

She tried to still the uneasy jump of her heart. "Is there something you're not telling me?"

He seemed to shake off whatever was bothering him and gave her his usual grin. "Nope. Just impatient, I guess. So tell me about the investigation."

Not totally reassured, Elizabeth told him everything she'd learned so far. Which wasn't very much, she had to admit. "I imagine everyone in the village is aware by now that I'm investigating the fire," she said, watching Earl pour her a glass of sherry. "From what I've heard, several people believe it was deliberately set."

Earl raised his eyebrows. "What about the police? Have they changed their minds about that?"

"Not as far as I know." Elizabeth raised her glass and clinked it against Earl's. "To the end of the war."

"A quick end to the war." He took a sip and put down his glass.

Elizabeth knew he wasn't overly fond of sherry, and she considered it very thoughtful of him to share a glass with her when he much preferred a good Scotch. "The thing is," she said, "I'm not entirely sure the locked door has any real bearing on the case at the moment. Which is why I'd really like to search Mr. McNally's office, or what's left of it, to see if I can find the key."

Earl frowned. "Didn't the police do a search of the area?"

"Not as far as I know. The firemen investigated the cause of the fire, and were satisfied it started in the bucket of rags. They would have no need to search the office, I suppose. Once George had the report that the fire was accidental, he had no reason to search it either. Dr. Sheridan found no keys on the body of Mr. McNally, so I would think, since the door was locked, the key would have to be in the office somewhere. In his desk, I would assume."

"And if it's not there—"

"It could well mean that someone locked the door from the outside and took the key with him. Which might be enough to convince George to conduct a proper investigation. That and the threatening letters, that is."

"The office must be quite a mess after the firemen got through with it."

"Well, Mr. Meadows did say the fire had taken hold. I'm

hoping I can still search the desk, at least. That would be the most logical place to keep keys, wouldn't it?"

She rather liked the way Earl was looking at her. "You'll need someone to help you with that," he said.

"Exactly what I was thinking." She took a sip of her sherry and set down her glass. "You did say you were grounded."

"I did, didn't I?" He looked amused. "It looks as if I have myself a date."

"Really?" She beamed at him. "You'll go with me?"

"Of course I'll go. You don't think I'm gonna let you go charging around a wrecked building without me, do you? You could get yourself in some serious trouble."

She laughed. "It wouldn't be the first time."

"Exactly what I'm talking about. I—" He broke off as the door opened.

Both he and Elizabeth stared expectantly at the open doorway, but no one appeared. After a long pause, Elizabeth said tentatively, "Martin?"

The butler's muffled voice sounded from outside the door. "Yes, madam."

Elizabeth exchanged baffled glances with Earl. "Do you need some help, Martin?" she called out.

"No, madam. I was simply wondering how to knock on the door with my hands full. Sadie opened the door for me, but the dratted girl rushed off without knocking."

Earl's lips twitched and Elizabeth shook her head at him. "There's no need to knock, Martin. We know you're there. You may come in."

"Thank you, madam." The butler shuffled in bearing a large tray.

Earl pushed his chair back and rose to his feet. "Let me take that," he said, holding out his hands.

"Thank you, sir, but I can manage. Please seat yourself. It is my place to wait on you."

Earl looked at Elizabeth, who flapped her hand at him in a signal to sit down. "Thank you, Martin," she said, hoping that the elderly gentleman would make it to the table without everything sliding off the tray, as had been known to happen now and then.

The huge tray wobbled precariously as Martin approached the table. Elizabeth could tell Earl was itching to jump up and grab it, but he showed great presence of mind by remaining in his seat.

It was important to her that Martin feel capable of doing his duty, even if she and Violet did have to secretly help him out at times. The butler had long ago lost his ability to fulfill all the obligations of his position. With his failing mind, however, it was essential that he still feel useful. Elizabeth was very much afraid that without that, he might lose his somewhat fragile hold on life, and would simply give up.

It made for some apprehensive moments at times, and this was definitely one of them. She sat holding her breath as his gnarled hands slowly lowered the tray to the table. One end of it nudged against a silver candlestick, in which a tall candle flickered.

The slender candlestick wobbled, causing the candle to tilt on its side. Wax dripped onto the white linen tablecloth, and for a moment it seemed as if the candle would fall to the table. Earl shot out his hand and caught it before it could topple over. He straightened it with a swift flick of his wrist and sat back, while Martin appeared not to notice anything amiss.

"This looks wonderful," Elizabeth exclaimed, with a grateful glance in Earl's direction. "It's been months since I've tasted a steak."

Having settled the tray on the table, Martin straightened his spine as far as it would go. "Will there be anything else, madam?"

"I think the major would like a glass of Scotch, Martin."

"Yes, madam. I shall return as quickly as possible."

"Take your time," Earl told him. "I'm not in a hurry."

"If you'll pardon me, sir," Martin said, as he shuffled toward the door, "it strikes me that you Americans are always in a hurry about something. It took us almost two thousand years to perfect the English language, and yet the Americans took less than a hundred years to mangle it sufficiently enough to make it unrecognizable."

Elizabeth gave Earl a sheepish smile as the door closed behind her butler. "I apologize for that," she said. "You never know when Martin is going to deliver one of his cynical remarks. I'm sure he didn't mean anything personal by it."

Earl unfolded his serviette and laid it on his knee. "I'd just like to know what the villagers have against Americans."

"I'm afraid there are some people who have never quite forgiven the Americans for abandoning their country to stage a revolution."

He looked at her in surprise. "That was almost two hundred years ago."

She smiled. "We British tend to carry a grudge."

"You can say that again." He reached for her hand and covered it with his own. "I hope I never do anything to get you mad at me. I'd hate to wait two hundred years for you to forgive me."

She laughed. "That's not likely to happen. Now, let's enjoy this delicious steak before it gets cold. Look, Violet has baked a potato for you. She knows how you love baked potatoes."

"At least she doesn't hate the Americans."

"Nobody hates the Americans, really. They just don't understand them, that's all."

He withdrew his hand, and his face was serious when he asked, "What about you? Do you understand us?"

Again she felt that stab of apprehension. She had an idea that there was more to the question than it seemed, and she didn't want to worry about this now. The future was shadowy. It seemed as if she'd be tempting fate to put her hopes and dreams on such an uncertain outcome. One day at a time. That's all anyone could ask for.

She made her voice light when she answered him. "I think I understand *you*, and that's all that concerns me right now."

He nodded, apparently satisfied. Relieved, Elizabeth changed the subject to a mundane discussion of the weather. One day she would have to face the difficult decisions. But not now. Not yet. She would worry about that when the time came.

Having made arrangements with Earl to visit the factory that afternoon, Elizabeth decided the next morning to pay a visit to the daughter of Jessie Bandini. Conscious as always of doing the right thing, she felt she needed to offer comfort and assistance, even though she hadn't known the dead woman personally.

The funerals for both Douglas McNally and Jessie were to be held that weekend, and Elizabeth wanted to offer her sympathy to the daughter before the service, since she wasn't planning to attend.

She set off early that morning, grateful for the watery sun that peeked from behind straggly clouds. The snow was turning into dirty, wet piles of slush at the sides of the road, and little rivulets of water indicated that it was beginning to melt at last.

Normally Elizabeth would have been ecstatic at the prospect, but now came the unbidden thought that if the weather improved, Earl would no longer be grounded. As always, the thought of him taking to the skies filled her with dread. How terrible it would be, after all that had happened between them, to lose him now.

Determined not to let herself dwell on that, she took the coast road past the village, heading for Salishay Point. She could see the lighthouse in the distance, a lone white column with its glass hat staring out to sea on the very edge of the cliffs.

Just beyond that lay Quimby's farm, and the fallow field where Zora Bandini lived with her baby in a caravan. Elizabeth felt sorry for the poor girl. How dreadful to lose a mother, and the sole supporter for her and the baby. How alone she must feel.

She spotted the caravan as soon as she entered the narrow lane that led to the field. The garish red, yellow, and blue paint was faded, and a broken wheel caused the vehicle to lean on one side. A thin column of smoke rising from the tin chimney on top reassured Elizabeth that at the very least the baby was keeping warm.

She parked her motorcycle and pushed the creaking gate open. Carrying the basket of food she'd brought with her, she walked toward the caravan. Iron pots and a frying pan dangled from nails driven clumsily into the walls, and empty flower pots hung in front of the door. Behind the caravan, a clothesline had been strung from a corner to a pole stuck in the ground, and a line of nappies flapped in the breeze. Zora Bandini was apparently taking good care of her baby.

The door to the caravan was high off the ground, and

Elizabeth rapped on the lower half of it with her gloved knuckles. After a long moment, the door inched open, and a pair of dark eyes peered down at her.

"Good morning," Elizabeth said cheerfully. "You must be Zora Bandini. I'm Lady Elizabeth from the Manor House, and I've brought you some provisions you might be able to use."

Zora's eyes widened, and the young woman pulled open the door. "I wasn't expecting visitors, your ladyship." She waved a hand at the space behind her. "It's not very tidy in here." A tiny voice wailed from somewhere inside and Zora added hastily, "Beg your pardon. The baby's crying."

"I'd love to see the child," Elizabeth said. She held out the basket. "I'm really quite used to an untidy house. You should see my conservatory when the dogs have finished romping around in there."

A reluctant smile tugged at the girl's mouth, and Elizabeth was struck by her beauty. Her jet black hair hung straight and smooth down her back, and her proud nose and full lips were framed by a perfectly heart-shaped face. "Well, if you don't mind the mess . . ." She bent down to take the basket. "This is most kind of you, your ladyship."

Having been relieved of her burden, Elizabeth mounted the rickety steps. There was no handrail, and she felt a little insecure as she balanced on them, but she reached the door without mishap and stepped inside.

The lack of room inside the caravan took her breath away. A black pot-bellied stove with a large kettle sitting on top of it was crammed into one corner. A small dresser stood in the other. The table was no wider than two planks and was hinged to the wall to fold down when not in use. Two folding chairs leaned against it. Bunk beds lined the opposite wall, and on the floor in front of the stove lay a wooden cradle which rocked gently back and forth as the baby inside beat the air with her hands and feet to the accompaniment of her lusty howl.

Zora bent down and swept the baby up in her arms. The child immediately stopped crying. Bobbing her daughter up and down in her arms, the young woman said tentatively, "Can I get you something? I don't have much to offer, but pr'aps a cup of tea?"

"Thank you, I would love a cup of tea." Elizabeth held out her arms. "May I?"

Zora nodded and thrust the baby at her. Then she grabbed one of the chairs, unfolded it, and sat it in front of the stove. "There," she said, "that should keep you warm enough."

Elizabeth sat down, marveling at the creature in her lap. The child had dark hair, but unlike her mother, lighter streaks shone in the soft down. "How old is she?" Elizabeth asked, watching in awe as the small fist uncurled.

"Almost six months, m'm." Zora poured water from a large jug into the black kettle and sat it back on the stove.

"She must be a great comfort to you."

"She is." Zora's voice trembled slightly, and she crossed to the dresser and took out two cups and saucers.

"I'm so very sorry for the loss of your mother," Elizabeth said quietly. "I can only imagine how hard it is for you to cope without her."

The girl had her back to her, and merely nodded.

Guessing she was trying to compose herself, Elizabeth went on, "If there's anything I can do to help . . ." She paused, an idea coming to her. "For instance, I do happen to have a cottage vacant right now. It's close enough to the village that you could walk to the shops, and you could have it rent free until you get better situated. I'm sure you could find work in the village and—"

Zora turned so swiftly she made Elizabeth jump. "That's very kind of you, your ladyship, but I'm getting along all right. Farmer Quimby and his wife have been very good to me and I'm going back to work on the farm next week."

"Oh." Somewhat disappointed, though she couldn't say why, Elizabeth looked down at the child in her arms. "But what about your daughter? You can't leave her alone here."

"No, m'm. I wouldn't dream of doing such a thing. Mrs. Quimby will watch Loretta while I do me jobs."

Elizabeth glanced around the cramped confines of the caravan. "But don't you think you would be better off in a nice cottage closer to the village?"

Zora's lips thinned. "They don't like gypsies in the village," she said bluntly. "They say we bring trouble with us wherever we go."

"That's nonsense. I'm sure—"

"Begging your pardon, m'm, but Loretta and me belong here, in the caravan. It was good enough for me mum, and it's good enough for me."

Afraid she'd offended the girl, Elizabeth said hastily, "Oh, I didn't mean . . ." She let the words trail off. She wasn't sure what she had meant. She was well aware of the people's prejudice against gypsies, and what it would mean for Zora to fly in the face of convention. She would not be accepted joyfully, that much was certain. Yet she felt compelled to help the girl, as if somehow, it was her fault Zora's mother had lost her life. Which was ridiculous, of course.

Deciding it was time to change the subject, she said briskly, "Well, if there's anything I can do to help, please let me know."

"Thank you, m'm. But Loretta and me will be quite all right." Zora lifted the other chair and unfolded it. "It will take a while for the kettle to boil. I hope you don't mind waiting."

"Not at all." Elizabeth smiled as the baby gurgled. "I do believe she's trying to speak to me."

Zora sat down on the chair and held out her arms. "I'll take her now."

Reluctantly, Elizabeth handed over the child. "She must miss your mother."

Zora looked surprised at that. "Yes, I suppose she does. I never thought about that."

Her lower lip trembled, and Elizabeth said gently, "I'm sure you miss her, too."

"I tried to talk her into leaving that job, that's what breaks my heart." Zora laid her cheek on her baby's head for a moment. "I didn't like her working in that place late at night all by herself. Especially after she told me about the rumors."

Elizabeth frowned. "Rumors? What about?"

"The rumors about the guns being stolen and shipped to London."

Confused, Elizabeth stared at her. "I hadn't heard anything about that. What did your mother say about it, exactly?"

Zora shrugged. "Not much. I don't think she knew a lot. She just said that she'd heard that someone was planning to steal the guns and ship them to London to be sold on the street. I think she was afraid she'd get into trouble. The bobbies are hard on gypsies if they catch them breaking the law."

"Did she say who the someone was?"

"No, m'm, she didn't tell me." The baby whimpered, and Zora held her up. "I think she needs changing, if you'll excuse me."

"Of course." Deep in thought, Elizabeth held out her hands to the stove to warm them.

Behind her, Zora lifted the hinged table and snapped it into place. "I wanted me mum to stay home with the baby, and I said I'd get a job in the factory. But me mum said they wouldn't give me a job unless it was cleaning, like her. I said I'd do the cleaning at night, and she could stay home with the baby, but she said as how she was getting a big raise and she kept telling me to stop worrying about it. That everything was going to turn out all right. Then the next thing I know . . ." Her voice broke, and she struggled to continue. "The next thing I know," she said at last, "was that she'd died in a fire at the factory. I knew she'd come to a bad end there. I kept warning her, but she wouldn't listen."

"I'm so sorry." Steam rose from the spout of the kettle and Elizabeth stood up to reach for it. "Here, I'll make the tea." Pouring boiling water into the brown teapot Zora pointed to, she said quietly, "I'd like to visit you now and then, if you don't mind. You and Loretta."

She looked up to see Zora smiling at her, though tears glistened on her long, dark lashes. "We'd like that, wouldn't we, Loretta? That's very kind of you. We don't get many visitors."

The baby waved a tiny fist at her, and Elizabeth felt a surge of tenderness. There was just something about a baby . . . She stifled the longing before it took hold. She'd accepted the fact a long time ago that she'd never have a child. "You have a beautiful daughter, Zora," she said softly. "Take good care of her."

"Oh, I will, m'm. Don't you worry about that." Much to Elizabeth's delight, Zora handed the baby back to her. "Now let's have a nice cup of tea."

CHAPTER

❧ 12 ❧

When Elizabeth arrived back at the manor a while later, Martin greeted her with the news that she had a visitor waiting in the library. Her first flare of hope that it might be Earl arriving early for their appointment faded as she entered the room to find Fred Shepperton waiting for her.

He seemed ill-at-ease when he saw her, and couldn't quite meet her gaze. He declined her offer of refreshment, saying he was expected back at the farm for the midday meal. "I wanted to come and tell you this, your ladyship," he said, twisting his soft felt hat around until it was completely crushed, "before you heard it anywhere else."

Elizabeth regarded him gravely. "I do hope it's not more bad news."

"Oh, no, m'm. Not exactly, anyway. See, it's like this."

He looked down at the hat as if wondering how it had become so mangled. "I talked to Lydia when she got back from the cottage. I told her as how you were asking about the letters to McNally, and that you thought I might have written them. I told her you might think I set that fire and all."

"Well," Elizabeth said awkwardly, "I wasn't exactly accusing you . . ."

"No, let me finish." Shepperton cleared his throat. "The thing is, I recognized the printing on the paper soon as you showed it to me. I'd seen it enough times before. On the price tags Lydia puts on her tea cozies in the garden fetes. When I came right out and told her, well, she had to spit it out, didn't she.".

Somewhat confused, Elizabeth said warily, "I don't quite follow your meaning."

"Ah, well . . ." Shepperton coughed. "Well, it was Lydia, don't you see. She wrote them letters. Got really het up about McNally poisoning the land with his factory so she wrote the letters hoping to scare him off."

Enlightened, Elizabeth said slowly, "Oh, I see."

"I'm really sorry, your ladyship. She didn't mean any real harm, I'm sure. She just wanted to frighten the bloke off, that's all."

"Yes, well, it was rather a silly way to go about it, wasn't it."

"I reckon it was, m'm. I can tell you one thing, though. She didn't set that fire. That's a fact. My Lydia wouldn't hurt a fly. Besides, she was with me all day at the farm, and didn't leave to go anywhere. We went to bed together that night and she didn't get out of that bed until I got up after the explosion. I'm ready to swear to that on the Bible."

Elizabeth shook her head. "That won't be necessary,

Mr. Shepperton. I appreciate you taking the time to clear up the matter for me."

His face broke into a relieved smile. "Yes, m'm. My pleasure, I'm sure." He moved to the door. "I'm sorry for any trouble my wife might have caused. Like I said, she didn't mean no harm. She was really upset when she heard as how McNally had died. Felt like she wished it on him, she did."

Elizabeth was of the opinion that the woman deserved to feel guilty, but she refrained from saying as much. She rang for Martin to show the farmer out, but ended up seeing Shepperton to the door herself when the butler failed to appear. She was closing the door when Martin's testy voice sounded behind her.

"Pardon me, madam, but I do believe that it is my duty to show visitors the door."

"So it is, Martin." Elizabeth smiled at him. "Do forgive me. I quite forgot."

He eyed her suspiciously. "The master will be most displeased. He does not approve of your disregard for the dictates of your position."

"The master's dead, Martin," Elizabeth murmured automatically. Her mind was still dwelling on her conversation with Zora Bandini. The revelation that Lydia Shepperton had written the threatening letters had not exactly come as a huge surprise. After what Zora had told her about the rumors, she was beginning to suspect that the letters had nothing to do with the fire at the factory after all.

She was inclined to think it had more to do with illegally shipping arms to London. Could she possibly have misjudged McNally? Perhaps he had arranged to meet someone at the factory to arrange delivery of the illegal weapons. It would certainly explain why he chose to go back there late at night.

Now she was more anxious than ever to search the factory. She might well find more than a missing key, now that she knew what to look for and where to find it.

Impatient for her meeting with Earl, she left Martin standing in the hallway and headed for the kitchen stairs. He would follow at his own pace, she knew quite well, and she wasn't prepared to wait for him to navigate the stairs.

The warmth of the kitchen, heated by the old-fashioned stove in the corner, was a welcome change from the drafty corridor. Polly and Sadie sat at the large scrubbed wood table, and both of them jumped to their feet as Elizabeth entered.

Violet was busily stirring something on the stove and barely looked up when the girls greeted Elizabeth. "Oh, there you are," she said. "I was about to send out a search party."

"Am I that late?" Elizabeth glanced up at the clock. "I was talking to Fred Shepperton and didn't realize the time."

"I was wondering who the visitor was. I heard the bell ringing, but by the time I'd dropped what I was doing and washed and dried my hands, Martin had made it to the door." Violet turned something over in the pan with a spattering and sizzling of grease.

"That smells delicious." Elizabeth sat down on her chair, signaling for the girls to sit as well.

"Bangers," Polly said, sniffing the air. "They always smell good. Especially when you're hungry. Bangers and mash. My favorite dinner."

"Everything's your favorite dinner," Sadie said, nudging

her with her elbow. "I bet you're only saying that so's Vi will give you more."

"I'll thank you to call me by my proper name, young lady." Violet brought a plate over to the table piled high with fat pork sausages. She offered them to Elizabeth, who speared one with the serving fork and dropped it on her plate.

Violet laid the dish on the table for the girls to help themselves, then she went back to the stove.

"Did Ray make the poster for you?" Elizabeth asked, as Polly reached for a sausage.

"Yes, he did, m'm, thank you."

"Got torn off the wall, though, didn't it," Sadie muttered.

Elizabeth stared at her in concern. "Someone tore your poster off the wall?"

Sadie nodded. "See, there were a punch-up down the pub last night."

"Oh, no." Elizabeth groaned. "Not again. I was rather hoping things were settling down at the Tudor Arms."

Sadie lifted a sausage from the dish and flipped it onto her plate. "Nah. As long as you have Yanks and Limeys drinking together in the same pub you're going to have trouble. Human nature, ain't it."

Violet returned to the table with a steaming bowl of mashed potatoes. "Well, I can't see why they can't get along together," she said, dumping the bowl on the table. "After all, they're fighting the same war. You'd think they'd be supporting each other instead of bashing each other's noses in."

Sadie lifted the bowl and offered it to Elizabeth. "Not as long as the Yanks keep stealing the local girls, they won't."

"Well, surely there's enough girls to go around for all of them?"

Sadie's raucous laugh rang out. "What girl in her right mind wants to go out with a Limey when she can go out with a Yank?"

"I'd say they're more trustworthy," Violet said, earning a warning scowl from Elizabeth.

"Trust has got nothing to do with it. The Yanks have all the money."

Violet sat down in her chair with a thump. "Well, that's a mercenary reason for picking a young man if I ever heard one."

"It's not just the money," Polly piped up. "They're different, that's all. They're like . . ." she struggled with her thoughts for a moment, then finished in a rush, "film stars. That's what they're like. Glamorous, like the film stars."

"Yeah," Sadie agreed, nodding her head. "Everything's so much more exciting with them. They come from exciting places and do smashing things, like surfing on the ocean, and climbing mountains. Things we could never do here."

"They make us feel different," Polly added. "Like we're film stars, too. Yeah, they treat us like we're special, just like film stars. That's what's different."

Having listened with great interest, Elizabeth felt compelled to say, "I thought you'd decided not to associate with the Americans, Polly, now that you've met a nice English young man like Ray Muggins."

Polly shrugged. "I did. Ray's all right, I suppose, but after going out with Sam, he seems so . . . boring."

"Everyone would seem boring after Sam," Sadie said.

"Good great heavens!"

The voice from the door startled them all. All four heads turned in that direction.

Martin stood in the doorway, holding onto the frame for support.

Feeling guilty at having forgotten about him for the moment, Elizabeth asked anxiously, "Are you all right, Martin?"

"I am just a little out of breath, madam. I descended the stairs a little too fast."

Since it had taken him all this time to get to the kitchen, Elizabeth had to wonder where he'd still be if he hadn't hurried himself. "Well," she said, "come and sit down while the food is still warm. There's nothing more unpalatable than cold mashed potatoes."

"I will be honored to join you, madam, on condition that we have no more talk about fraternizing with servicemen. I find the subject thoroughly disgusting. These men should be utilizing their energy to fight the Germans instead of hobnobbing with local hussies. The master would never allow his staff to behave in such a despicable manner. I shall have a word with him about it."

"The master's dead," Elizabeth and Violet said in unison. They had long ago decided that if they repeated the fact often enough, Martin would eventually accept it. So far, however, he showed no signs of doing so.

"Here he goes again." Sadie waved her fork at him. "Just watch who you're calling a hussy, mate. I'll have you know that Polly and me always act proper, and we've never done any frat . . . frater . . . whatever it was you said."

"Fraternizing," Violet snapped. "I wish you wouldn't talk to Martin with your mouth full and in that uncouth manner. Show some respect for your elders."

"I will when he shows some bloody respect for me," Sadie mumbled.

Violet reached out and cuffed Sadie's ear.

"Ow!" Sadie glared at her, but Violet had already turned her back.

Apparently appeased by Violet's support, Martin shuffled over to the table. Addressing Elizabeth, he said in his usual pompous manner, "May I have your permission to join you at the table, madam?"

Well used to the habitual ceremony, Elizabeth said graciously, "Of course, Martin. Please sit down."

"Thank you, madam."

"Not at all." Aware that Sadie and Polly were doing their best to keep a straight face, she added, "If you're finished with your meal, ladies, you may be excused."

To her relief, both Sadie and Polly rose to their feet. Mealtimes could sometimes be too boisterous with everyone seated around the table.

Violet put a plate down in front of Martin then sat down herself. Martin looked at the dish of sausages with a disagreeable frown. "Sausages again? When are we going to have a decent roast? A leg of lamb with mint sauce, or pork with apple sauce would make a nice change."

"Go and tell that to the butcher." Violet split open her sausage and piled mashed potatoes in between the two halves. "I haven't seen a nice joint in there for months. I reckon he keeps what he wants for himself, and doles the rest of it out to his favorite customers."

"I saw two or three joints of beef when I was in there yesterday," Elizabeth murmured.

Violet looked at her in surprise. "What were you doing in the butcher's shop? You can't get much in there without coupons and I've got all the ration books in my room."

"I was asking Jack Mitchum some questions." Annoyed with herself, Elizabeth immediately regretted the slip. So far she'd managed to keep quiet about her investigation, knowing how much Violet worried about her getting involved in police business.

Violet narrowed her eyes. "I heard in the village you were asking a lot of questions about the fire at the factory. You think someone set fire to it on purpose, don't you."

"I was wondering if perhaps the three musketeers were at work again," Elizabeth admitted. "I do wish the constables could catch those hooligans. They've caused so much damage in the area."

"Don't they have any ideas who it might be?"

Elizabeth swirled her fork in her mashed potatoes to make a pattern. "The only clue we have is the Royal Air Force badge I found last year. I find it hard to believe that British airmen are responsible for cutting tires on American Jeeps and leaving nails in the road to disrupt their lorries, much less setting fire to a factory and causing the death of two people. I would think they had more important things to worry about than this silly rivalry with the Americans."

"Not so silly when two people get killed," Violet said soberly.

"No, you're quite right." Elizabeth put down her knife and fork. "This is a very serious situation. Something must be done to find out who caused the fire."

"What about George and Sid? What are they doing about it?"

"The fire chief's report states that it was an accident, and George is quite happy to accept that."

"But you're not."

"No, I'm not." She looked up to meet Violet's penetrating stare. "I can't say why at this point, Violet, but I'm convinced the fire was set deliberately, and that whoever set it knew Mr. McNally was in that office."

Violet gasped. "You're saying someone wanted Douglas McNally dead?"

"A lot of people wanted him dead," Martin said, making them both jump.

"What do you know about it?" Violet demanded. "Have you been talking to that raffle lady again?"

"If you are referring to Beatrice Carr," Martin said haughtily, "then please say so and refrain from referring to her as a raffle lady."

Elizabeth shook her head at Violet, then asked Martin, "What did Beatrice say about Mr. McNally?"

The butler carefully pushed the last piece of sausage onto the back of his fork and lifted it to his mouth. He chewed for agonizing seconds before swallowing, then he said smugly, "Mrs. Carr told me that most of the villagers wished that Mr. McNally had never come to Sitting Marsh. They were worried that he would change the village into a town like North Horsham, with all those infernal motorcars belching out smoke and deafening people with their horns and noisy engines. They were also afraid the Germans would bomb us out of existence."

"But did Mrs. Carr say anything specific about the fire?" Elizabeth persisted.

"She said it was a pity the fire brigade got there so soon. She would rather the whole building had burned to the ground rather than just the roof."

Elizabeth stared at him. His words had triggered that odd feeling again, though she couldn't imagine why. Martin hadn't told her anything she didn't already know.

Then again, that was usually the way things turned out. So many times when she'd been investigating a murder, the missing piece of the puzzle was something she already knew and just hadn't put it all together. She had that same feeling now. Somewhere in all the information she'd gathered was the missing piece of the puzzle. All she had to do was put a finger on it.

"Well," Violet said, as she reached for the empty plates, "I just hope you don't get yourself in trouble again, Lizzie. You have a bad habit of putting your nose where it doesn't belong. One of these days you might get it bitten off if you're not careful."

"I'm always careful." Elizabeth got to her feet. "Besides, I'll have the major with me this afternoon when I go up to take a look at the factory. So you can stop worrying about me, Violet. I'll be in good hands."

"That's a matter of opinion," Martin muttered, struggling to get out of his chair.

Elizabeth gave him a stern look. "Really Martin, I fail to see that it's any of your business."

"Quite right, madam. Quite right. I was merely making a comment. Please excuse me if I was out of place."

"You're always out of place," Violet said, rolling her eyes at Elizabeth. "Even if you are right."

For once Elizabeth could not let things lie. "I'm getting extremely tired of defending my relationship with Major Monroe," she said sharply. "I'll thank both of you to remember your position and keep your noses out of my business."

Violet seemed startled, while Martin simply looked tired. "Lizzie," Violet began, but Elizabeth interrupted her.

"Enough. I really don't feel like discussing the subject any more. I shall be gone this afternoon and will return in time for supper. If anyone needs me, please tell them I shall be available this evening." She left the room quickly, before she gave in to the impulse to apologize for her outburst. For once she felt justified, and she could only hope that both Violet and Martin would think twice before making such adverse comments again.

She was in the office when a light tap on the door broke her concentration. Polly lifted her head and gave her an enquiring look.

"It's all right, Polly," Elizabeth said, rising from her chair. "That will be Major Monroe. He's taking me out to look at the factory. Just finish those letters to the residents for me, and then you can leave."

Polly nodded. "Thank you, m'm. There's something important I have to do tonight. I'll be glad of the extra time to get ready."

Elizabeth barely heard her. She was already halfway out the door, her heart thumping with anticipation. It didn't seem possible that such a short time ago she was contemplating life without ever seeing Earl again. And now here he was, standing right here in the hallway, looking at her with a smile that made her heart sing.

"Hi there," he said softly. "How's my girl?"

She closed the door quickly, afraid Polly would hear. "Your girl," she said, with mock severity, "would prefer that you not address her as such in front of the servants."

He held up his hands. "Sorry, I forgot."

She smiled up at him. "It's good to see you."

"It's always good to see you." He linked his arm though hers. "Ready for our tour of the factory?"

"Indeed I am. Just let me get my coat and scarf. Riding in that Jeep of yours can be so ghastly chilly."

He raised his eyebrows. "It can't be any worse than riding on that motorcycle of yours."

"Perhaps not, but then I don't travel with such reckless speed on my motorcycle."

"Are you criticizing my driving?"

"I wouldn't dream of it," Elizabeth assured him as they descended the stairs together. "Let us just say that the British drive with far more decorum and a greater respect for the correct side of the road." ·

"More decorum." He appeared to think about that. "I guess that's because you're more used to driving a horse and cart than a motor vehicle."

She uttered a sigh. "This is why I enjoy a discussion with you. You have such an antiquated and biased view of the English people. I find it quite refreshing."

He burst out laughing. "Elizabeth, you are the only person I've ever met who can make an insult sound like a compliment. You'll have to teach me how to do that sometime."

"I will, if you promise to teach me how to drive that deplorable Jeep."

"I seem to remember you handling that particular skill quite well on your own."

She wrinkled her nose at him. "If you are referring to the mad dash I took after a certain spy, I must remind you that I had no inkling of what I was doing. If you remember, I overturned the wretched thing and ended up in a ditch."

"I remember it well." He squeezed her arm with his. "You scared the heck out of me."

"So you will teach me to drive it properly?"

"You've got a deal." He held the door open for her. "Now let's go take a look at that factory before it get's too dark to see."

She stepped out into the weak sunlight of the wintry afternoon, happy to be going anywhere with him. *In fact,* she thought ruefully, *I'd follow him to the ends of the earth, if only I were anyone else other than Lady Elizabeth Hartleigh Compton, renowned lady of the manor.*

CHAPTER

❀ 13 ❀

"All right, ladies!" Rita Crumm clapped her hands to get everyone's attention. "It's time to hand in your signatures for the petition. Marge Gunther will add the numbers up for us, then I'll take it down to the next council meeting and present it to the councilors."

"I got twenty-six names," Marge boasted, waving a sheet of paper at the women sitting around Rita's front room. "I bet not many of you got that much."

"Twenty-nine," Nellie Smith called out.

"Thirty-one!" someone else shouted.

Marge looked put out. "All right, show-offs. Who else?"

"Sixteen!"

"Twenty-three!"

"Nineteen!"

"A hundred and four," a meek voice warbled.

A stunned hush filled the living room. Marge's hand slowly descended and she turned to the frightened-looking woman huddled in a corner. "Florrie? Florrie Evans, was that you?"

"Yes," Florrie admitted. She shot a wary look at Rita, who treated her to her stoniest stare.

"How many did you say?" Marge demanded.

Everyone stared at Florrie with varying degrees of expectation. Everyone knew that Rita had made signature collecting a competition, though no such words had actually been spoken.

Everyone also knew that Rita had collected forty-three names on her list, and that it would cost someone dearly if they dared to outdo this number. For that someone to be the most timid member of the Housewives League was even more impressive.

"I got a hundred and four names," Florrie said nervously. "Look, they're all here." The sheets of paper she held up rustled in her trembling hand.

"A hundred and *four?*" Marge's eyes appeared to be bulging from her head. "Where in heaven's name did you get that many signatures in two days?"

Florrie swallowed and stared around for help. Every woman in the room hastily looked away. "I'd rather not say," she said weakly.

Deciding it was time to take matters into her own hands, Rita strode across the room until she was practically standing on the unfortunate woman's toes. "You *have* to say," she said, fixing Florrie with a fierce glare. "We can't just accept names willy-nilly! You can't just walk in here and say you have a hundred and four names and not expect us to ask where you got them!" Despite her best efforts, her voice rose to a shriek. "Tell us where you got the blinking names!"

Florrie's mouth opened and shut like a baby sparrow's beak, but no sound came out.

"There's not that many grown-up people in the entire village," someone muttered.

"And we got most of them," Marge declared. "My full count is a hundred and eighty-seven counting Rita's forty-three. That's more than half the village."

Rita towered over the shaking woman, while Florrie seemed to shrivel up. "Florrie Evans, either you tell us where you got these names, or I tear up all these sheets." She snatched them from the woman's trembling hand and peered at the first page.

After scanning the first two or three names on the list, she wrinkled her brow. "Wait a minute. I don't recognize any of these people. Sydney Watkins? Jocelyn McTavish? Percy Codwall? Who are these people?"

"I went to North Horsham," Florrie said, her voice barely above a whisper.

Aware of several pairs of eyes on her, Rita swallowed hard. Forcing the words through her gritted teeth, she said slowly, "You went to North Horsham?"

Florrie nodded.

Rita's voice rose to a howl. "Who in blazes told you to go to North Horsham?"

Florrie looked as if she would burst into tears any minute.

"You never said not to," Marge pointed out helpfully.

Rita turned on her. "Mind your own bloody business!"

Marge simply shrugged, while the rest of the ladies appeared to be struggling to keep their faces straight.

With a great effort, Rita managed to get her temper under

control. Nobody outdid Rita Crumm. Nobody. But for now she would have to accept this measly little twerp's list, and make the best of it. After all, the more signatures they had, the better. "Very well, Florrie," she said painfully, "I will accept these signatures. "But next time, make sure you know all the rules before you go off doing things on your own."

The entire group broke into wild applause, only to be silenced almost immediately by Rita's baleful glare. It was a bitter pill to swallow, and not one she was likely to forget. She'd get even with that miserable twit in her own way. It would be a very long time before Florrie Evans dared to cross her again.

In spite of her warm scarf, the wind whipped across Elizabeth's face as Earl drove the Jeep along the coast road. White horses rode the greenish blue waves of the ocean, and a gray pall hung over the horizon, signaling another storm. It couldn't get there fast enough, as far as she was concerned. Storms kept the airmen grounded, and safe.

It was a miracle he hadn't had a mission that afternoon, considering the skies were fairly clear. She sneaked a glance at him. It was hard to tell what he was thinking. They rarely discussed his duties at the base. It was an unspoken agreement between them that she didn't ask questions. Now and again he'd volunteer whatever he wanted to tell her, but he always omitted details and specifics.

Churchill was constantly reminding the people that spies were everywhere, and it was essential not to discuss military or defense matters in case of being overheard. Idle chatter about such things could be helpful to the enemy.

She had to wonder how successful the people of Sitting Marsh would be keeping quiet about a munitions factory in their midst. With so many of the villagers working there, it

would have been almost impossible to keep anything secret, given the proficiency of the village grapevine. Perhaps the arsonist had done them a favor, after all.

She immediately dismissed that notion. Two people had
died in that fire. No matter what Douglas McNally had been
up to, he hadn't deserved to die in that gruesome manner. As
for Jessie Bandini, she was an innocent victim. Such a dreadful tragedy. Thinking of Zora and little Loretta, Elizabeth's
heart ached for them.

"You're looking very serious."

Earl's raised voice made her jump. They had to shout to
be heard above the engine and the wind that whipped words
from their mouths the instant they were spoken.

"I was thinking about the fire," she called back.

He sent her a brief glance. "Any ideas yet who might be
responsible?"

She shook her head, one hand holding onto her hat.
"Lots of people had motive enough to set the fire, but so far
all my suspects appear to be innocent."

"You don't think it's possible it could be an accident after all, like the fire chief says?"

"Anything's possible at this stage. That's why I want to
look for the key. If it's there, that will destroy my theory of
someone locking Mr. McNally into his office. On the other
hand, there's something I haven't told you yet."

He swung the wheel over to turn into the lane that led to
the factory. "What is it?"

"I went to visit Jessie Bandini's daughter this morning.
She told me her mother overheard rumors that someone
was planning to steal military weapons and ship them to
London."

This time his glance held concern. "Elizabeth, I hope
you know what you're getting yourself into."

She shrugged. "At the moment I really don't know much about anything."

Having reached the fence that guarded the factory, Earl slowed the Jeep and cut the engine. "If there's something like that going on, this could be very serious business." He turned to her. "You're not just talking about a prank getting out of hand. This is big time. With some pretty heavy criminals involved."

She felt a little nervous jump of her pulse. "Such as the three musketeers, for instance?"

He shook his head. "No, most of us believe they're just a public nuisance. I'm talking about someone much more dangerous."

She shifted uncomfortably on her seat. "Well, Jessie could have been quite wrong, of course. Then again—" She suddenly remembered something Zora had said, and caught her breath.

"What? What are you thinking?"

She turned to find his piercing gaze directed at her. "Zora told me that Jessie was expecting a big raise. But the factory had been open only a few weeks. Who would give a cleaning lady a raise after such a short time?"

"Maybe she threatened to quit and McNally couldn't find anyone else to clean his office, so he offered her a raise to stay on."

"That's possible." Elizabeth considered the idea.

"Okay, so now what's going on in that busy mind of yours?"

"I was just wondering," Elizabeth said slowly, "if Jessie told anyone else about the rumors."

Earl looked puzzled. "I don't follow you."

"What if the big raise she was expecting was actually

someone paying her to keep quiet about the rumors she heard?"

He stared at her, a frown creasing his forehead. "You mean blackmail?"

"Yes." Caught up in her excitement, she grabbed hold of his sleeve. "Supposing we've been concentrating on the wrong victim? What if someone were trying to get rid of Jesse Bandini, and it was Douglas McNally who was in the wrong place at the wrong time?"

"It's possible, I guess." He shook his head. "That doesn't explain what McNally was doing there so late that night. If the rumors about the weapons are true, I'd be more ready to believe that McNally was conducting some kind of illegal dealing and something went wrong. Maybe he was the one Jessie was blackmailing."

"Ray Muggins told me that he thought Mr. McNally went to the factory that night to make sure Captain Carbunkle wasn't sleeping on the job. Suppose he saw something he wasn't supposed to see. Maybe someone attacking Jessie, for instance. Wouldn't the killer have to get rid of him, too?"

"I guess so." His brow wrinkled in concentration. "Though how are you're going to prove that?"

"Perhaps by finding some evidence of the theft and who might be behind it. No one has searched the factory as yet. At least we know what we're looking for."

"Well, I guess we're not going to find out anything sitting here." He climbed out, then came around the bonnet to help her to the ground. "I'm just glad you asked me to come along with you this afternoon. I don't like the idea of you poking around here on your own."

"I'm glad you're here, too." She shivered, telling herself

it was the cold wind that chilled her. After all, it was broad daylight. Nothing alarming could happen to them, surely.

She followed Earl to the gate, which had been left unlocked. Apparently the constables had not deemed it necessary to safeguard the building now that it was in ruins.

It was the first time she'd seen the factory since the fire. Staring at the blackened walls and the huge, gaping hole in the roof, she felt sickened at the thought of those two helpless people, trapped inside the office while the deadly smoke filled the room.

Earl had reached the steps at the far end of the building, which seemed to have escaped most of the damage. He tried the door, but this time met with resistance. "Locked," he said briefly.

"Oh, dear." Elizabeth stared at the door as if she could will it to open. "We'll have to find another way in."

Earl glanced up at the shattered roof. "I don't think you should be going in there, anyway. What's left of the roof doesn't look too stable. It could collapse at any time."

Elizabeth nervously followed his gaze. "It shouldn't take more than a few minutes to search for the key. After all, there's not too many places a man would keep his keys while he's working."

"Well, if you insist, then I'll go in alone. You can wait for me in the Jeep."

"I'd rather go in with you than wait out here alone." She glanced around, her sense of uneasiness growing. "It feels so eerie here now that the factory is deserted."

Earl grinned. "You're not expecting to see Martin's ghosts, by any chance?"

She shuddered. "Heavens, I sincerely hope not."

"Come on, then, let's see if we can get in the other door."

Again she followed him as he marched to the other end of the building. This end had been severely damaged by the flames and the water administered by the firemen. The steps to the door were charred, but they held as Earl tested each one with his weight.

He reached the door and shoved his shoulder against it. It flew open, and a cloud of ash billowed out into the clean, crisp air. The dreadful odor of burned materials almost overwhelmed Elizabeth as she followed Earl inside.

Surrounded by blackened beams, she picked her way carefully across the charred floor, mindful of his warning to watch her step.

"Do you know where the office is?" Earl asked.

She pointed down the shattered hallway. "Mr. McNally took me there when he gave me a tour of the factory. It's down there on the left."

With a wary glance above his head, Earl proceeded down the hallway, with Elizabeth close on his heels. A few yards further he halted, and she almost bumped into him. "This must be it," he said.

Peering around him, she saw a door hanging drunkenly from one set of hinges. Beyond it, she could just see the corner of a desk, and file cabinets against the wall.

"Yes, it is!" She nudged him forward and followed him into the room. "It hardly looks burned at all. There's more water damage in here than anything." She glanced at the floor, where the force of the firemen's water hoses had swept papers, books, files, and boxes to the floor. She shuddered, thinking of Douglas McNally and Jessie Bandini. "Let's start looking," she said in a low voice.

"Good idea. Then we can get out of here. I'll take the desk." He stepped over the mess and started hunting through the clutter on the desk. A pile of soaked ledgers disintegrated when he picked them up. "We'll never be able to read these," he said, his voice tinged with disgust.

"Are there any keys laying around?" Elizabeth asked, stepping gingerly across the floor to the file cabinets.

"Nope, can't see any keys here," he said, as he stacked the soggy papers in a tray.

"Try the drawers," Elizabeth suggested. She approached a file cabinet and went up on her toes to look on top of it. She could see nothing but a thick layer of dust.

Behind her, she heard Earl opening and shutting drawers. "This one's locked," he muttered. "I don't think we're going to get it open."

"Can you force it open?" Elizabeth began picking her way toward him. Her path took her close to the window, which had miraculously remained intact. She glanced outside, noticing that the sun had disappeared behind some heavy clouds. The storm was moving in fast.

"I don't think we're going to find any keys," she said slowly. "Mr. McNally and Jessie must have heard the explosion. They would have gone to investigate if they could."

"Unless the smoke got to them before they could get out."

"But it must have taken some time for the smoke to reach this end of the building. According to Wally, it took him several minutes to get out of the building. He actually saw the roof collapse after he got outside. There should have been plenty of time for Mr. McNally and Jessie to leave the office. If not the building."

He looked at her. "It does look as if someone locked them in here so they couldn't get out."

"Then why didn't they leave by the window?"

He gave her a long stare. "Because they couldn't."

"Right." She made her way back to the window and looked out. "I'm convinced someone knocked them both out, then locked them in the office, hoping they wouldn't wake up in time to get out."

"It's possible, I guess. But I don't see how we're ever going to know for sure what really happened. It's all guesswork." He grunted, and she turned to see him prying the lock on the drawer with a paper knife.

"That must have been quite a sight, the roof caving in . . ." She broke off, staring hard at the window.

Behind her, she heard Earl exclaim, "Ah, got it!" There was a short pause, then he added, "But no keys."

"It doesn't matter," Elizabeth said quietly. "I think I know—"

Her words were cut off by a loud pop, followed by the sound of splintering glass. Stupidly she stared at the round hole in the window above her head. She could swear it wasn't there a moment ago. It had little lines spreading out from it like a jagged spider's web.

"Elizabeth!"

Something hit her in the back and she went down, stunned by the weight of Earl's body on top of her. Her breath knocked out of her, all she could do was whimper.

Earl eased his weight off her back, but still hovered over her. "Stay down," he ordered. "And don't move. That's an order."

Fighting to get her breath back, she was forming the words in her mind to tell him she didn't take orders from anyone. Not even him. But then he said something that swept the words away in a haze of shock.

"Someone's shooting at us," he said grimly. "We've got to get out of here."

"You going out with Joe again tonight?" Polly stared at Sadie. "This must be getting serious."

Sadie laughed. "Don't be daft. I wouldn't get serious over no Yank. You know better than that." She flopped down on her bed next to Polly. "Anyway, what brings you to my humble abode in the middle of the afternoon?"

Polly gazed at the calendar on the wall. It had a picture of the ocean on it, with palm trees on a long, sandy beach. "This is a nice room," she said, trying to imagine what it would be like to lie on a beach like that with someone. Like Sam.

"Yeah, I like it." Sadie gazed around in satisfaction. "Much better than the room I had in London. I was lucky to have this, though. When I was after the job here, Lady Elizabeth wanted me to have one of the cottages. I told her I'd rather live here. I don't think she would have agreed, though, if I hadn't told her about being bombed out of me home in London."

Polly looked at her, awed by the thought of actually talking to someone who had been bombed out. "That must have been awful," she said.

"Yeah, it was." Sadie's smile faded. "There was glass and bits of wood and plaster everywhere. Dust you wouldn't believe. I nearly choked to death before I crawled out of there."

"Wonder you weren't killed." Although she tried, Polly just couldn't picture what it must have been like. "I bet you were glad to get out of London."

"I was." Sadie sighed. "Though sometimes I miss it. There was always so much to do in London. Down here there's nothing except the pub and the pictures. That's why I go out with Joe. He's good company. Someone to spend time with. Even if he is as slow as a blinking snail."

"Better than having hands like an octopus," Polly said. She wasn't going to admit it to Sadie, but she really envied her friend. She missed the attention Sam used to pay her.

"What about Ray, then?" Sadie gave her a sly look. "How's he with his hands?"

Polly picked at the little knots of wool in the blanket beneath her. "He's all right. At least he stops when I tell him to."

Sadie lowered her head to look Polly in the face. "You don't sound very happy."

"I'm not." Relieved to get it out, Polly's words tumbled out in a rush. "I just don't want to be with him, that's all. I mean, he's nice and all, but he's not . . ." She let her voice trail off.

"He's not Sam," Sadie said, sounding a little impatient. "Polly, you've got to get over Sam. You're never going to have any fun in life if you're always pining over him. One day you'll want to get married and have kids and—"

"I wasn't going to say Sam," Polly said, butting in. "I know I've got to forget him. It's going to take time, that's all. Right now I don't feel like going out with anyone. Especially Ray Muggins. He bores me to death. Always talking about London, he is, and all the stuff he did when he was there. Keeps talking about all the girlfriends he had. I don't know why he stays down here if he likes the city so much. I wish he'd go back."

The last words had come out a little more fiercely than she'd meant. Sadie patted her on the shoulder. " 'Ere, 'ere. Don't go on like that. Why don't you break up with him if you don't want to go out with him anymore?"

Polly swallowed past the lump that had formed in her throat. "I think I will. I'll tell him tonight." She peeked up at Sadie. "I don't suppose you'd come with me, would you?"

Sadie frowned. "You afraid of him?"

Polly smiled nervously. "I dunno. I never broke up with someone before. I don't know what he'll say."

"Tell you what." Sadie got up from the bed and bent at the waist to peer in the dressing table mirror. "Tell Ray you want to go to the Tudor Arms tonight, and I'll get Joe to take me down there. You can break up with Ray, and me and Joe will be there to take you home."

Polly leapt to her feet and threw her arms around her friend. "Oh, thank you, Sadie. Thanks so much. I didn't know what I was going to do if he threw a fit. I'll feel so much better if you and Joe are there. I'll go and ring him right now."

"That's settled, then." Sadie grinned at her friend. "By tonight you'll be a free woman again."

Polly smiled. She felt as if a load had been lifted from her shoulders. A free woman. That sounded good. That sounded really, really good.

CHAPTER

❈ 14 ❈

"Who do you think it is?" Elizabeth whispered.

"I don't know." Earl cautiously raised his shoulders to peer over the windowsill. "But I sure aim to find out. Do you know anyone who owns a gun?"

"Some of the farmers might have a shotgun, but otherwise I know of no one in the village who would have one. This isn't America, you know. There are pretty strict rules about who owns a gun. Even the constables don't have one."

"That was no shotgun. That was a rifle, by the look of that bullet embedded in the wall."

"Military?"

He glanced down at her. "Could be."

"Stolen from here, perhaps?"

"I wouldn't be surprised." He raised his head higher.

"Be careful!" She pulled him down again. "He's probably still out there. He'll shoot again."

"Just stay down."

To her dismay he edged away from her and crawled over to the window. She watched him straighten up, his back pressed against the wall. "I'll say one thing. The shooter was a lousy marksman. The bullet hit way above your head."

"Please get away from that window!" Elizabeth pleaded. "He might not miss next time." She sat up and examined her knees. "Drat. I have ladders in both stockings."

"And that's why they don't let women in the trenches," Earl said, a trifle too smugly for Elizabeth's liking.

Offended, she glared at him. "What does that mean?"

"I'll tell you later. Right now I have to get you out of here without getting your head shot off."

She scrambled to her feet. "That's not in the least amusing."

"It wasn't meant to be."

She uttered a little shriek as he grabbed her arm and pulled her up against him. "I wouldn't advise you to stand in front of the window like that. You make a perfect target."

She wasn't sure what was the most unnerving—the thought of a gunman trying to kill them or being clamped against Earl's chest. Fortunately for her peace of mind, he pushed her away from him. "Stay there and don't move until I say so."

Right at that moment she doubted that she could move if she tried. She watched Earl pick up a piece of wood and wave it in front of the window. Tensed for another bullet to hit the glass, it was almost anticlimactic when he let the board drop to the floor.

"Well, at least he's stopped shooting at the window. Too bad they took all the weapons out of this place after the fire. I sure could use a gun right now." He looked at her. "Are you ready to make a run for it?"

Her stomach muscles clenched in fear, but she nodded at him. "Ready."

"That's my girl." He took hold of her arm. "Just do exactly as I say, and if I yell, you drop like a stone. Immediately. Got that?"

She knew now why he was considered such a good leader. The order had been given firmly, but with confidence and reassurance in his voice. She felt safe with him, sure that he would get her through anything unscathed. "I'm ready," she said steadily.

"Good, then let's go. Keep your head down as we go past the windows. We'll go out the locked door at this end. It's closer to the Jeep."

"What if we can't unlock it?"

"I'll break it open. Under the circumstances, I think the owner would understand."

It occurred to her then that she didn't know who owned the building. Douglas McNally had merely been the manager. He'd never told her who his employer might be. She assumed the owner would be down to look at the building before too long, since he planned to rebuild.

They reached the door without incident. Earl paused in front of it and looked down at her. "Elizabeth, the gunman could be waiting outside for us. I'm gonna to do my best to get us both out of here, but if something happens to me, you make it to the Jeep on your own. You don't wait for me, got it?"

"But—"

Gently he laid a finger on her mouth. "No buts. You promise me. You remember how to get it started?"

Miserably she nodded. "I think so."

"Then you take that Jeep and you go straight to the pub. It's not that far. You can call the police station from there."

"I don't want to go without you."

"With any luck you won't have to. Now you promise me. Please."

She struggled with her reluctance a moment longer, but his stern expression warned her he would take no less. "I promise," she said weakly. "But under protest."

"Noted." He stroked her face before pulling his hand away. "Stay real close to me, okay?"

"All right." She watched him try the lock, then heave his shoulder against the door.

It didn't budge, and he looked around for something to force it. "Well, look at this," he said softly.

She peered around his shoulder to see what he was looking at. On the wall was a row of pegs, and hanging from the pegs were several keys.

"What's the betting this is where McNally kept the keys to the office," Earl said, reaching up to take one down. "That's how our intruder got a hold of it." He fitted the key into the lock on the door, but it wouldn't turn.

Elizabeth grabbed the rest of the keys off the pegs and handed to them. "One of them must fit."

The third one he tried turned smoothly in the lock and he let out a sigh of satisfaction. "Now, let's see if our gunman's out there. Stay here, Elizabeth. Don't move until I tell you. When I give the word, run like hell for the Jeep."

She nodded, too scared now to speak.

Earl inched the door open, and she held her breath as he poked his head outside. Any second she expected to hear a shot. Her heart was pounding so hard it shook her body.

He pulled back inside again and looked down at her. "I'm going to step outside. Get ready to run."

Her feet felt as if they were fastened to the floor. She prayed she'd be able to move when he gave the word. He started forward and she grabbed his sleeve.

"Wait! Earl . . . if anything happens . . . I . . ." She couldn't say it after all. Fear had dried up the words.

"Me too." he said softly.

Weak with the knowledge that he'd read her mind, she watched him step into the graying dusk. Every nerve in her body screamed with tension. Blood pounded through her veins, throbbing in her head, her ears, behind her eyes.

He was outside now—vulnerable, facing a deadly danger.

She'd worried about him before, every moment she knew he could be on a mission. But then it had been a danger she couldn't see, a faceless enemy, a vague ache of wondering where he was and when he'd return.

This was different. This was immediate and right in front of her. He was risking his life to save hers. She opened her mouth to call him back, but before she could utter a sound he snapped an order at her.

"Run! Go! Go! *Go!*"

She plunged through the door and he grabbed her hand. Together they leapt down the steps and raced across the yard to the gate. Any minute she expected to hear the deadly sound of a gunshot and wondered, ridiculously, how much it would hurt to have a bullet thud into her defenseless back.

They were at the gate now, and her lungs heaved painfully for air. Earl thrust her through, then practically threw her into the Jeep. "Get down!"

She scrunched down as much as she could as Earl leapt over the side and into his seat. The engine fired on the first try, and then they were off, careening around in a wild circle before heading back down the road to safety.

It wasn't until they were racing down the driveway of

the Manor House that she felt able to draw a deep breath again. As Earl helped her out of the Jeep, she was shaking so hard she wasn't sure her knees would hold her up.

"Brandy," he said, as they mounted the steps to the door. "And then we call the police."

Too weak to argue, she leaned against him as they waited for Martin to open the door. "I can't believe someone was actually trying to kill us."

"I'm not so sure about that."

She looked up at him in surprise. "What do you mean?"

"I think he was just trying to frighten us off. He missed you by a mile in the window, and he could have easily waited around until we left the building to take a better shot at us."

"So it was a warning?"

"A pretty effective one at that. From now on you let the police do the investigating. I don't want you taking any more risks."

She pursed her lips. He was awfully fond of giving orders. She was about to remind him that she wasn't one of his men to be bossed around, but just then the sound of bolts being slid back heralded Martin's tardy arrival at the door. *Later,* she promised herself. When she felt more calm. Major Monroe needed to learn that she was used to doing things her own way, and didn't take kindly to someone trying to dictate her life. Even if she was madly in love with him.

The brandy went a long way to soothe Elizabeth's rattled nerves, but there was no time to confront Earl about his well-intended but unwelcome supervision. He was in a great hurry to inform the police about the shooting, and he rang them from her office, much to Polly's avid excitement.

"They want me to go down and fill out a report," he said,

when he replaced the receiver in its cradle. "I'm due back at the base shortly, so I'll run down there now."

"Do you want me to come, too?" Elizabeth asked, hoping he'd decline. There was much to do in the office, and all this running around had put her behind. She'd promised Polly she could go home early, and she could tell her assistant was in a hurry to leave.

"There's no need," Earl said, heading for the door. "If I go on my own I can go straight to the base from the police station. I've got some stuff to catch up on this evening."

"Very well, then." Feeling guilty for causing him to work late, she followed him to the door. "Can you see yourself out?"

"Sure." He smiled at her. "You did great out there. I'm proud of you."

"I was scared to death," she admitted.

"I know. But you didn't lose your head. That took guts."

Warmed by the praise, she said quietly, "Thank you. But if it hadn't been for you, I think I'd still be in there, cowering like a frightened mouse."

Aware of Polly hanging onto every word, she was relieved when he turned to leave with a lift of his hand. "So long. I'll be back later."

She closed the door behind him and leaned on it for a moment. Now that it was all over, she was reliving the horror of those frantic moments. It all seemed so unreal, as if it had happened to someone else. It was hard to believe that she'd been shot at as she'd stood in that window.

She frowned, trying to remember that moment more clearly. She'd been thinking about something important at the time. Something significant that had now annoyingly slipped her memory again.

"Are you all right, m'm? You must have had a terrible shock."

Polly's voice jerked her out of her thoughts. "Yes, just a little shaken, that's all." She managed a light laugh as she turned to face her assistant. "Why don't you run along now, Polly. I believe you said you were doing something important tonight."

"Yes, m'm, I am. I'm meeting Ray tonight."

"Oh, how nice!" Elizabeth gave her a warm smile. "I'm so glad you're getting along so well with that young man."

"Yes, well, as a matter of fact, m'm, I was going to tell you—"

The telephone rang at that moment, cutting off whatever she was going to say. Elizabeth reached for it, and said, "I'll take this. You have a nice evening, Polly. Don't stay out too late. I don't want to see you falling asleep over your desk tomorrow."

"Yes, m'm. I mean no, m'm. I mean . . . thank you . . . m'm."

Polly rushed from the room and Elizabeth frowned. Her assistant seemed a little agitated. Probably upset about the news of the shooting. As well she might be. Speaking cautiously into the handset, she said, "The Manor House. Lady Elizabeth speaking."

The familiar female voice that answered her sounded surprised. "Good afternoon, Lady Elizabeth! This is Nellie Smith. I was expecting Polly to answer."

"Polly had to leave, Nellie," Elizabeth told her. "Is there something I can do for you?"

"Well, actually, it was Polly I wanted to speak to. I saw her poster in the pub, and I was wondering if she had any names of lonely soldiers yet so I can write to them."

"Ah, yes, Polly did mention something about that. I think

she's waiting to hear from her sister. I believe she's meeting her young man tonight, but she'll be here tomorrow. Perhaps you can ask her then."

"Oh, right. She's going out with that Ray Muggins, isn't she."

Something in Nellie's tone sharpened Elizabeth's interest. "You are acquainted with the young man?"

"I've met him, yeah."

"You don't like him?"

Nellie hesitated, then said carefully, "Well, I don't know him that well, m'm, but he seems a bit shifty to me. Can't look you straight in the eye. My dad used to say if they can't look you in the eye when they're talking to you they got something to hide."

Elizabeth's fingers tightened on the handset. "Well, I'm sure Polly will use her common sense when it comes to her relationship. Meanwhile, I'll tell her you rang, and that you'll be in touch with her later."

She replaced the handset and leaned back in her chair. Thinking back to her conversation with Ray Muggins, she remembered the way he'd looked everywhere but directly at her. Why hadn't she noticed that at the time?

She sat up straight in her chair. Now she remembered what she'd been thinking about when the bullet had come through the window. Now it was all falling into place. She sat there for a long time until she was sure she had it straight in her mind.

She thought back to her first conversation with Ray Muggins, on the stairs. He'd been so upset about Douglas McNally's death. He'd told her how he'd left the Tudor Arms and arrived at the factory in time to see the roof cave in. Sparks shooting up like rockets, he'd told her. But Wally had also seen the roof collapse. *Before* he'd bumped into Fred

Shepperton on his way back from the pub. Which meant that Ray couldn't have followed the farmer back to the factory. He was already there.

It was small thing. But why would Ray Muggins lie? There could only be one reason.

If he had been the one shooting at her earlier, he probably had the rifle hidden in his room. She had to search his room. She had to make sure before she raised the alarm.

Polly. She was going out with him tonight. For a moment Elizabeth considered warning the child. But to do that would raise Ray's suspicions. He'd realize someone suspected him and he'd disappear before she could convince George to arrest him.

She glanced up the clock. Almost half-past four. Polly wasn't likely to meet Ray until seven or so. She had a few hours to get through before she could leave for the pub.

She stared at the telephone, wondering if she could ask Earl to go with her. No, she'd taken up enough of his time. Already he was having to catch up on work he'd neglected in order to take her to the factory.

After all, she'd be perfectly safe. Ray's room was at the Tudor Arms. It was just a matter of slipping up the back stairs, a quick search of the room, then down again.

In any case, she wasn't sure that her suspicions were founded. She just knew that something about Ray's story didn't add up, and she was reluctant to question him about it. If she was right, then she could be dealing with a very dangerous criminal.

Part of her nagged that Earl would want her to go to the constables with her suspicions. But knowing George, he'd hem and haw, tell her she was relying too much on guesses, and perhaps botch things up as he always did, allowing Ray Muggins to slip away unchallenged.

She couldn't let that happen. Two people had died, and someone had to pay for their deaths. She needed some kind of proof, however, before she presented her case, and if her hunch was correct, searching Ray's room just might give it to her.

Ray would be out with Polly this evening. Knowing Polly and her passion for films, they would most likely go to the cinema in North Horsham. That would give her plenty of time to go to the Tudor Arms, conduct her search, and be safely away before Ray returned to his room.

Having decided that, she went down to the kitchen to ask Violet to prepare the evening meal a little early. She wanted to make sure she had plenty of time for her mission.

Polly walked into the lounge bar of the Tudor Arms, wishing she could be anywhere rather than the noisy, smelly pub. Normally she didn't mind the stink of beer and the choking smell of cigarette smoke. But there were times when it got on her nerves.

Thank goodness Sadie couldn't afford to smoke. At least she didn't have to put up with the smell in the manor. Polly glanced around the crowded room. No sign of Ray at the bar, and she couldn't see him at any of the tables. No sign of Sadie and Joe, either, which unnerved her a bit.

Still, there was plenty of time. She sauntered over to the bar, ignoring the comments from both GIs and British soldiers as they jostled each other to get close enough to order their beer.

All the bar stools were occupied, but a pimply faced Yank jumped up and offered her his seat, his face turning scarlet at the sly remarks of his mates.

Polly thanked him and slid onto the stool. Alfie was at

the other end of the bar. He caught her eye and gave her a little wave, then went on pulling pints as fast as he could.

He needed another barmaid, Polly thought, feeling sorry for the bloke. The last one he had turned out to be a German spy, and since then, he hadn't had much luck finding anyone to work behind the bar. Most of the local girls would rather be in front of it, having a good time with the Yanks.

It seemed ages before Alfie paused in front of her just long enough to ask, "The usual, luv?"

She nodded, glancing once more in the mirror that ran the length of the bar. She could see the door from there, and to her relief, she saw Sadie come in, followed by her red-headed boyfriend, second-lieutenant Joe Hanson, United States Army Air Force.

Polly grinned, thinking of the number of times Sadie had given him his full title when she mentioned him. She watched them sit at a table over by the window, and once more she felt a pang of envy. Joe seemed nice. And he was a Yank. How she missed being with an American. But those days were over, she told herself. No more Americans in her life. No Yank was ever going to break her heart again.

Elizabeth waited quite a while before she felt it safe to slip up the back stairs of the pub. Fortunately, the back door had been left unlocked, as usual, so she hadn't had to go through the bar. If all went well she could leave again without even Alfie knowing she'd been there, which would certainly help her to avoid having to answer some awkward questions.

Alfie had once confided in her that he kept a spare set of keys in a drawer in the hallstand. She'd thought at the time that it wasn't a very prudent place to keep keys. Then again, the drawer did blend into the ornate carving on the front of the hallstand. Most people wouldn't even notice it was there.

Alfie had chosen to leave the keys there to save him going back into his room to get them when someone forgot their own key, which happened far too often in Alfie's estimation. Elizabeth was very glad now that he'd shared that bit of information. Little had she known at the time how useful it would be.

She knew where to find Ray's room. The only one with a view of the ocean, he'd told her. Everyone knew that was room number one. Visitors usually asked for it when they booked a room at the pub.

She had almost reached the top of the stairs when she heard a door open further down the hallway. She paused, praying it wouldn't be someone who recognized her. The rooms were mostly let out to visitors from out of town. Even so, she was quite a prominent figure around the village.

She risked a quick peek around the corner. To her horror she recognized the man strolling toward her. It was Ray Muggins. He had to be on his way to meet Polly.

Immediately she turned and fled for the stairs. He'd had his head down, as usual. The hallway was dark and shadowy. With any luck she could duck out of sight before he saw her.

Leaping down the stairs, she twisted her ankle painfully as she reached the bottom. The outside door was just a few steps away and she raced for it as Ray's footsteps clumped down the stairs behind her. Frantically she tugged the door open and plunged outside. Breathing hard, she walked rapidly away from the pub, expecting any minute to hear him calling out to her.

When she reached the corner without hearing the dreaded shout, she risked a glance over her shoulder. There was no one there. He must have gone into the lounge bar to meet Polly.

Obviously she'd misjudged the time. Polly's meeting with Ray was later than she'd thought. It was too late for them to go to North Horsham now, so that meant they were probably spending the evening in the pub.

Racked with indecision, she stood poised on the corner. One half of her wanted desperately to go home and wait until tomorrow when Earl could go with her to search the room. Then again, knowing Earl, he'd try to talk her out of it.

Also, if Ray was the gunman, he might know she was on his track. And there was nothing to prevent him from leaving Sitting Marsh and disappearing into the busy streets of London. He could be gone before they found out anything useful.

No, it had to be tonight. Ray and Polly would spend at least a couple of hours in the lounge bar. They might even leave to go somewhere else. Pulling another deep breath, Elizabeth walked cautiously back to the pub.

CHAPTER
❊15❊

"Well, there you are!"

Ray's soft voice made Polly jump. She'd been staring at Sadie and Joe so hard she hadn't noticed him come up behind her. She looked at his reflection in the mirror. "You're late," she said, but he wasn't listening. He was too busy trying to get Alfie's attention.

"I'm going to find a table," she told him, sliding off the stool. "Alfie's getting my gin and orange."

She left Ray at the bar and went in search of a table. Most of them had been taken already, but she found one close to the door. No one liked sitting that close to the door in the winter. Every time someone came in, the wind cut into your legs and froze your toes.

Tonight, however, she didn't plan on being there too

long. She'd have one drink with Ray, then tell him it was over. Her stomach churned at the thought.

Anxiously, she stared across the room at Sadie, who was nose to nose with Joe talking about something. You had to get that close in this place if you wanted to say something without everyone near you overhearing it.

Her stomach jerked again when she caught sight of Ray making his way toward her, her gin and orange in one hand and a glass of beer in the other. It was now-or-never time.

She wished now that she'd rehearsed what she was going to say. She'd never done this before. How was she going to tell him without hurting him, or worse, making him angry? She should have talked to Sadie about it. Sadie always knew what to say.

Polly glanced over at Sadie's table again. It was too late now. Sadie and Joe were sitting there waiting for her to finish it with Ray so they could take her home. She'd ridden her bicycle down there, but Joe could throw it in the back of his Jeep. It was better than riding in the dark.

Ray reached the table and put the glasses down. Foam slopped over the side of his glass and spread in a little puddle on the table. Polly watched it, wishing she could just jump up, tell him it was over, and rush out of the pub.

Somehow she got through the next fifteen minutes, though she had no idea what they talked about. It was mostly Ray talking, while she mumbled answers. It usually was Ray who did all the talking, she realized now. They'd never had a real conversation, like she and Sam used to have.

"You wanna another one?" Ray asked, breaking into her thoughts.

"No, thanks." Now was the time, she told herself. Now,

before he bought her another drink. While she still had enough guts to go through with it. She glanced over at Sadie, just to make sure she was still there.

Sadie was watching her, and gave her a thumbs up sign. That made her feel better. Ray started to get up, and in a sudden panic, she said loudly, "Sit down, Ray."

He paused halfway off his chair, his eyes widening. "What?"

She'd never spoken to him like that before, she thought nervously. No wonder he was surprised. "I've got something to say to you," she said. "I want you to sit down so you can listen."

Slowly he put down his glass and lowered himself onto the chair. "What's all this about?"

"It's about you and me." Polly swallowed. Her heart was banging so hard against her ribs she could hardly get the words out. She sent a frantic glance at Sadie, who was still watching her. She saw Sadie say something to Joe and he turned his head to look across the room at her.

Polly drew a deep breath. "I'm not going out with you anymore, Ray. I want to break up with you."

The look in his eyes frightened her. "What's the matter?" he said, in a harsh voice she'd never heard him use before. "Not good enough for you? Is that it?"

Scared now, she shook her head. "No, it's nothing like that. I just don't think we're right for each other, that's all."

He started getting to his feet again. "So you want to go back to being Yankee bait, is that it?"

Tears stung her eyes, but she gritted her teeth and blinked them back. "I'm sorry, Ray, I—"

"Sorry!" He leaned toward her, frightening her even more. "I'll make you sorry, all right, you little—"

"Is everything all right, Polly?"

Joe's voice had cut across Ray's words, and he straightened up. "Mind your own business—" Ray started, but that was as far as he got.

Joe's hand closed around his throat. "This *is* my business," he said quietly. "If I were you, I'd go right out the door. Unless you want to take on that whole squadron over there." He jerked his head at the bar.

Ray dragged Joe's hand from his neck. "I'm going," he said nastily, "but I'll be back. With my own squadron. So watch your step, Yank." With one last baleful glance at Polly, he charged out the door.

One quick look, Elizabeth promised herself, and she'd leave. If she did find something incriminating, it would be a simple matter to go down to the bar and ask Alfie to ring George. He'd be there before Ray knew anything was amiss.

Assuring herself that she had plenty of time, she nevertheless scurried up the steps, her spine tingling at the thought that he could be waiting for her to come back. She reached the upper hallway, and with a quick glance confirmed that she was alone.

She hurried toward the room, unlocked it with the key, and slipped inside. After closing the door, she scrabbled in the dark to find the light switch and turn it on. Bright light flooded the room, making her blink.

She didn't have to look far after all. It was in the wardrobe, more or less where she'd expected to find it. The lethal-looking rifle was propped up in one corner, behind a suit of clothes.

So she was right. Ray Muggins had shot at her this afternoon. If her guess was right, he was the one involved in the theft of guns. The person whom Jessie Bandini had been foolish enough to blackmail.

She had to get to George's house and bring him back here before Ray realized he'd been discovered. She started to close the wardrobe, but at that moment, the door opened behind her.

Frozen with shock, she could only stare at Ray's astonished face, knowing that whatever she said would not explain her presence there, or why she was looking in his wardrobe.

Already his surprise had turned to comprehension. For once he was staring right at her, and the menace in his eyes was frightening.

He stepped inside the room and closed the door behind him. "Well, well. Very clever, your ladyship," he said, in a voice she didn't recognize. "How'd you know it was me?"

He stepped toward her, and she backed away from the wardrobe in an effort to put the bed between them. "I was looking for Polly," she said, doing her best to sound normal. "I thought she had an appointment with you this evening."

He grinned, and she wondered why she'd ever thought him pleasant and charming. "She did, but she decided to go home early. Too bad you didn't try the lounge bar first. You'd have run right into her."

He moved closer to the wardrobe and she swallowed hard. "Oh, I did look in there and didn't see her. It's so crowded down there tonight."

"A little too crowded I'm thinking." He reached inside the wardrobe and drew out the rifle. "Then again, with all the noise going on down there, no one would hear this if it were to . . . accidentally go off. Right?" Very carefully, he pointed the gun at her and positioned his finger over the trigger.

She stared at the menacing mouth of the barrel, her stomach threatening to return the contents of her hastily eaten meal. A voice shouted inside her head: *Don't let him see you're scared!* But it wasn't that simple. *All very well,* she thought desperately. Something urged her to keep him talking. Anything to play for time. Maybe someone would come down the hallway and she could yell for help.

"You know very well you can't shoot that thing off in here," she said, trying her best to sound confident. "Alfie will hear it if no one else does. He'll come right up here to find out what's going on."

"Maybe you're right."

To her immense relief he withdrew his finger. "Perhaps we should go for a little ride."

"I don't think so." She fought to keep her voice calm. "I'm supposed to meet someone in the bar in a couple of minutes. If I'm not there he'll come looking for me."

Ray's eyes narrowed. "You're lying."

"Can you afford to take that chance?"

"I don't have any choice." He gestured with the rifle. "Let's go."

"I'm not going anywhere," Elizabeth said bravely.

"All right, then. I suppose I'll just have to take the chance no one hears this." He raised the rifle again and once more his finger hovered dangerously close to the trigger.

"You don't have to do this, you know." Elizabeth sought frantically in her mind for the right thing to say. "I'm sure you didn't know that Mr. McNally and Jessie were in the building when you set fire to it. The police will take that into consideration, I'm sure."

His cruel gaze raked her face. "What makes you think I set the fire?"

She swallowed. "Captain Carbunkle saw the roof collapse

before he went for help. On the way he met Fred Shepperton, who was on his way back from here. Since you were in bed when Mr. Shepperton woke you up with his call to the police station, you had to be at least five or ten minutes behind him in leaving here. Yet you described in detail the roof collapsing. That meant that you were already at the factory when Captain Carbunkle escaped from the building. There was only one reason why you would lie about that. You killed Douglas McNally, didn't you?"

Ray's face seemed to shrivel up. "I didn't know Douglas was going to be there. It was Jessie I was after. She found out something she shouldn't, and she wanted me to pay her to keep quiet. I couldn't take the chance that she'd spill the beans." He gave her a fierce glare. "That's the trouble with women. They don't know how to keep their mouths shut about anything."

Elizabeth's skin crawled. "How did she find out?"

He gave her a piercing look. "She heard me talking on the telephone, didn't she?"

"To your contacts in London?"

His eyes narrowed. "How'd you know about that?"

"I know you were stealing weapons from the factory and planning to ship them to London. I assume you have contacts there to buy them. But what I don't understand is why you came all the way down here to steal them. Surely there are munitions factories closer to London?"

"Maybe there are," he said nastily, "but things were getting too hot for me in the city. That's why I was in this sodding miserable hole in the first place. I decided to move my operations down here to the middle of nowhere. Far away from anyone who might know what was going on."

"So this isn't the first time you've stolen guns and sold them illegally."

His laugh was pure menace. "Lady, everyone has a way of making a living. This is mine, that's all."

"And I presume there's nothing wrong with your heart, is there."

He looked puzzled for a moment. "My heart?" Then his frown cleared. "Oh, Polly told you. She wanted to know why I wasn't in the army. I had to tell her something to keep her quiet."

"Of course," Elizabeth said quietly. "After all, Mr. McNally would never have hired a deserter."

A flash of anger crossed Ray's face. "Conscientious objector, if you don't mind. Anyway, none of this is any of your business. Not that you're going to live long enough to tell the tale." He raised the rifle again.

"There's just one more thing I don't understand," Elizabeth said, keeping her gaze steadily on his face. "If you didn't plan on killing Mr. McNally, when you found him there, why didn't you just wait until the next night to deal with Jessie? Why did you have to kill them both?"

He stared at her for a long moment and she saw a moment of real regret in his eyes. "He saw me. I clocked out that night and hid in the men's toilets at closing time, waiting for Jessie. I thought she'd do the toilets first, but when she didn't turn up I got tired of waiting. I saw her in Douglas's office. I hit her on the head with a hammer. When I turned around to leave, Douglas was standing in the doorway." His voice broke and he took a ragged breath. "He wasn't supposed to be there. I didn't have a choice. He'd seen me hit Jessie. I had to get him, too."

She could almost feel sorry for him, realizing how much Douglas McNally had meant to this twisted young man. "So you locked them both in the office."

Ray shrugged. "What else could I do? I went back and

got the keys, locked the office in case they woke up, then set fire to the bucket of rags. I thought the whole place would burn down and no one would ever know what happened to them. The bloody thing went up so fast I almost didn't get out myself."

"Ray," Elizabeth said gently, "I'll go with you to the police station and help you explain . . ."

"Don't be stupid." Ray aimed the rifle at her again. "No one's going to hear me shoot you, and even if they do, by the time they realize what's going on I'll be long gone from here."

"I don't think so," a voice said from the doorway.

Elizabeth stared in wild relief and amazement as Earl rushed into the room, with Alfie close behind him. Ray swung around, but Earl knocked the rifle from his hands and it fell with a clatter to the floor. Alfie pounced on Ray and between them the two men wrestled the struggling young man to the bed, where Alfie sat on him.

Close to tears, Elizabeth gazed at Earl, thinking she'd never seen such a glorious sight in her entire life.

"You all right?" he said roughly, striding toward her.

She nodded weakly, but still had the presence of mind to warn him with a little shake of her head as he looked ready to clasp her in his arms.

She could see the frustration in his eyes, but he dropped his arms and went back to pick up the rifle. His voice sounded ragged when he asked Alfie, "Can you hold him?"

Alfie nodded. "George is on his way with the cuffs. He'll be here pretty soon."

"I'll wait with you till he gets here." Earl turned back to Elizabeth. "You look like you could use a drink. Why don't you go down to the bar and wait for me down there. I'll pay for it when I come down."

She didn't want to leave his side. She never wanted to leave his side again. "How did you know where I was?"

"I didn't." He exchanged a grim look with Alfie. "I stopped by to see if you wanted to share a nightcap with me. Violet said you'd gone out. She was worried. You don't usually go out on your motorbike in the dark. So I said I'd look for you. This was my first stop. I saw your motorbike in the parking lot."

So much for keeping my visit a secret, Elizabeth thought wryly. Anyone seeing her infamous steed would know she wasn't too far away. That hadn't even occurred to her. "I'm not much of a detective," she said ruefully.

"The major came into the bar and asked me where you were," Alfie put in, shifting his position as Ray struggled beneath him. He flicked the young man's ear with his fingers. "Stay still," he ordered gruffly, "or I'll make sure you can't move."

Ray grunted something unintelligible.

"I saw Polly and Sadie," Earl said, "and they said they hadn't seen you. That's when I figured you were up to something. Alfie went to get the keys to the rooms and they were missing. We came up here and heard him . . ." he gestured at Ray ". . . threatening you. That's when we stepped in."

Words could not express her relief and gratitude. All she could manage was a weak, "Thank you. Both of you. You saved my life."

"I'll have something to say about that later," Earl promised.

She rather liked the masterful way he said that. "I'm sure you will," she murmured. She looked anxiously at Alfie. "If you're up here, who's tending the bar?"

Alfie grinned. "I commandeered your housemaid," he said cheerfully. "And your assistant and her boyfriend.

There's not a lot of skill in pulling a pint, and we don't have much else down there right now."

Heavy footsteps sounded in the hall, and a gruff voice called out, "You in there, Alfie?"

The next few minutes went by in a flurry of questions and explanations. Ray stubbornly refused to talk, so Elizabeth filled in the gaps. Then George clapped the handcuffs on Ray and led him away.

"Reckon I'd better go and see how them young'uns are doing behind my bar," Alfie said, and he followed George and his sullen prisoner down the stairs.

"We'd better get out of here, too," Earl said grimly, "before I'm tempted to forget my promise about keeping my distance. But one thing I am going to say. If you ever do something like this again, I'll personally see to it that your detecting days are over."

Elizabeth looked him steadily in the eye. "And just how do you propose to do that?" she asked demurely.

"There are ways," Earl muttered, taking hold of her arm. "Believe me, there are ways."

She was tempted to ask him for more details, but she thought better of it. Instead, she went with him into the cool, dark night, secure in the knowledge that no matter what scrapes she might get into, he would always be there for her. What more could a woman want?

Meet Captain Gabriel Lacey in

The
Hanover Square
Affair
by
Ashley Gardner

IN WAR OR AT PEACE,
CAPTAIN LACEY KNOWS HIS DUTY.

His military career may have ended with an
injustice, but former cavalry officer Gabriel Lacey
refuses to allow others to share his fate.
The disappearance of a beautiful young woman
sets Lacey on the trail of an enigmatic
crime lord—and into a murder investigation.

0-425-19330-6

Also in the Regency England Mystery series:
A Regimental Murder
0-425-19612-7

Available wherever books are sold or at
www.penguin.com